A Stairway to Paradise

Born in Sydney, Madeleine St John graduated from Sydney
University and has since lived mostly in London. Her third
novel, *The Essence of the Thing*, was shortlisted for the 1997
Booker Prize. Her other novels are *The Women in Black*
(1993) and *A Pure Clear Light* (1995).

A Stairway to Paradise

★

MADELEINE ST JOHN

FOURTH ESTATE • *London*

This paperback edition first published in 2000
First published in Great Britain in 1999 by
Fourth Estate Limited
6 Salem Road
London W2 4BU
www.4thestate.co.uk

1 3 5 7 9 10 8 6 4 2

A catalogue record for this book is available from the
British Library.

ISBN 1–85702–888–0

Typeset by Avon Dataset Ltd, Bidford on Avon B50 4JH
Printed in Great Britain by Clays Ltd, St Ives plc

For Kathy Kettler

PART I

I

Barbara for some reason insisted on sitting in the back, so she got in first, ducking past the front passenger seat and then thumping herself down; and sitting there, arrayed, with her large bag – what the hell was she carrying around? – beside her: great, she said. This is just great.

And then the two men got in, Andrew sitting where she ought to have sat, his long legs hunched up uncomfortably, but half-turned around to face Barbara, as if politely not wishing to have his back towards her, because he was well, he was *impeccably*, brought up, was Andrew: Andrew's manners were sometimes enough to bring tears to your eyes.

So he was sitting there in the front passenger seat, half-turned towards big velvety Barbara in the back, when Alex got in behind the wheel, even more hunched up than Andrew.

'This your vehicle, is it, sir?' said Barbara to the back of Alex's head. She knew perfectly well that it was actually Claire's weeny run-around: but Andrew didn't know that she knew, because Andrew knew, precisely, *rien*.

Alex simply grunted and turned on the ignition. But then he paused a moment. 'Who's first?' he said. 'Well—' said Barbara. 'I suppose it had better be you,' said Alex. 'My sentiments entirely,' said Barbara. 'Rev her up then, gov.' Alex, silent, let out the clutch and drove off. Barbara knew that silence. Barbara knew the exact meaning of the present set of that neck, the tension it harboured, the quality of the explosion to come. Ah well, she thought. Not my *problème*. She waited until they were crossing Battersea Bridge before she spoke again. 'Is there by any chance a sound system in this motor?' she asked. 'No,' said Alex shortly. 'Oh, well,' said Barbara airily. 'Never mind.' And she began to sing.

> There's a saying old, says that love is blind
> Still we're often told, seek and ye shall find . . .

And so it went on, through Chelsea, South Ken, the Park, Paddington, and so on, northwards – you know the route – all the way to bloody Belsize Park: a good big intolerable slice of the George Gershwin songbook. Andrew's long legs were half asleep by the time they reached Barbara's house; stiff with cramp he got out of the car and waited for Barbara and her big bag to emerge. 'Well,' she exclaimed. 'Here we are indeed! I won't ask you in – hope you don't mind. Terribly late.' She bent over and looked at Alex through the open door: he was sitting rigid, mute, over the wheel, just waiting. 'Good night, lover,' she said. 'Thanks for the ride. I'll do the same for you some time. Take care!' She straightened up: Andrew still stood, waiting to re-enter the car. 'Good night . . . er,' she said. 'Andrew.' 'Good night, Barbara,' he stuttered. Oh, God, if I could just ask her for her telephone number – I can't. Impossible. *Oh, God.* And she's gone. He got back into the car, demoralised, in a turmoil. *There's a somebody I'm longing to see . . .*

Now they were on their way to Islington, through the bright half-empty two a.m. streets, in silence, each

4

possessed by his own ghostly, ghastly confusion of thought and emotion.

'You'd better direct me from the Angel,' said Alex, 'okay?' 'Right, right,' said unhappy Andrew. Here now was the Angel. 'Right here. Now second left.' And so it went on. 'Just past that Volvo.' The car stopped. Andrew turned to his friend, his old, old friend from Oxford days, whom he hadn't seen now for ten years. Andrew had just returned from ten years' teaching in the United States, and his broken American marriage. Sadness and failure, sorrow and grief. And his little American child whom he would now see once a year, for a month in the summer. Failure and grief. Pick up the threads of the old life, the old English life – English life: sweet, sweet rice pudding, lumpy and sweet and deceptively bland: except that it wasn't there any more, not that sweet, sweet pudding he'd thought he remembered, no, not quite, no, not really: no, not at all. Was it? See the old friends: the dear old friends, their manners deceptively bland, their values deceptively relative, their wits like long sharp needles: except that they too weren't quite there, any more; they weren't quite where he thought he remembered their having been. Nothing was as he'd thought it would be; he was just trying, now, to find a place where he could get a foothold, a piece of ground one could actually put one's foot on, stand on, without going under, the water over one's head: he'd been back here for, what, three months, and he was still treading water, trying to find the ground under his feet. Alex, now. He, at any rate, was still married to Claire (but now had two children) and still worked in Fleet Street. Which wasn't in Fleet Street any more.

2

Alex craned his neck and looked up at the façade of the house. 'Which bit is you?' he said. 'Have you got the first?' 'The second and third,' said Andrew. 'Thought I might as well have two bedrooms. For when Mimi comes over, and so on.' There was a moment of cold, painful, saddened silence. 'Yes, of course,' said Alex. 'Won't you come in for a moment?' said Andrew. 'If you're not too shattered.' Alex hardly liked to refuse, in the circumstances. That cold, painful sadness. 'Not a bit,' he said.

There were the two men, hovering about vaguely in Andrew's brand-new rather empty sitting-room: a battered chesterfield (very expensive), an armchair, a coffee table: the *Eye*, *The Economist* and the *Independent*. Alex picked up the last by a corner. 'Oh, you read this thing, do you?' he said with a wry smile. 'Well,' said Andrew. 'Thought I ought to catch up. It's new since I went away.' 'Like everything,' said Alex. 'And nothing.' 'Ye-e-es,' said Andrew. 'Everything. And nothing.' Oh, God, he thought. He was in perpetual pain. But he was brave, brave, brave. 'Barbara, for example,' he said.

'Barbara?'

'Isn't she new?' asked Andrew. Alex's face might have seemed to darken for an instant, even to show unease, but Andrew was not looking at it: Andrew was looking sidelong at the floor, because Andrew did not want Alex

7

to see the avidity with which he was pursuing this topic shining from his eyes; Andrew did not want Alex to know what he was feeling about Barbara.

'Not very,' said Alex. 'Well, new since your day, of course. Technically speaking. Well, perhaps actually speaking too. Yes, very possibly. All right, she's new. The absolutely modern, the truly contemporary woman. How do you like her?'

Undressed, said Andrew to himself. He almost laughed at the pleasantry; almost laughed with delight at the idea of undressing Barbara and helping himself to what he would then find. Her skin was so smooth, so golden. She had lustrous golden-brown hair. Careful, careful. He was too busy with his thoughts and their concealment to notice his friend's tone and the perturbation it betrayed; still now he was avoiding Alex's gaze, filling the electric kettle, getting some mugs from a cupboard in the galley kitchen at one partitioned-off end of the sitting-room. 'She seems . . . well . . . new.' She's as new as the dawn. 'Interesting. She tells me she's never, ever, had *a proper job*. Remarkable.'

'It's just a generational thing,' said Alex dismissively. 'Graduate unemployment, and so on.' 'No, but – I mean, how does she manage?' 'Oh, ask her,' said Alex drily. He could bear no more of this. 'Oh, well,' said Andrew. 'I mean – do you know her well?' 'Hardly at all,' said Alex. 'She's more Claire's – well, friend isn't *quite* the word, I dare say. They used to see each other a fairish bit, a few years ago. Not so much now I think. Perhaps not at all. I hardly know her.'

'What's that place where she lives?' asked Andrew. 'Looks rather a good address for someone without a job.' Alex laughed. 'Oh, you'd be surprised,' he said. 'The benefits system here is really interesting.' He laughed again.

8

'As it happens, however,' he said, 'she has in fact a sort of job at the time of speaking. The flat in Belsize Park is a tied cottage. She cooks and cleans for the people in the house. She gets the basement flat rent-free in return. Plus they pay her fuel bills. Not bad going.' Andrew laughed. 'So she's a servant,' he said. 'Yes,' said Alex. They both laughed. 'Some servant,' said Andrew. They laughed again. They were both in pretty desperate need of laughter at this juncture, were these two.

'Does she sing for them?' asked Andrew. More laughter. Alex stopped laughing. 'No, she only does that when she wants to annoy *me*,' he said. Andrew looked at him. 'I thought you said you hardly knew her,' he said. They were both sitting down now and Alex was making a spliff. 'So I did,' said Alex; 'so I did.' He licked the gummed edge and fastened the whole thing up. 'Here you go,' he said, and he handed it to his host. Andrew went to the kitchen and fetched the matches. He took a drag and handed it back to Alex. What was going on? Who was watching over whom?

'How is Claire?' he asked. Alex took a while before answering. 'As I told you,' he said. 'She's fine. She's fine, is Claire.' 'Pity she missed the party,' said Andrew. 'Sorry not to see her there.' 'Well, you can't have everything,' said Alex. 'Not even Claire can have everything. Can't go on holiday to Brittany *and* go to a party in Battersea at the same time. Isn't a reasonable proposition.' 'Maybe she's been at a party in Brittany,' said Andrew. 'Yes, why not?' said Alex. 'Well, but – do they have parties in Brittany? Doesn't sound likely to me. What do you think? Did you ever hear of a party in Brittany? Ever get asked to one?' 'I suppose those hats would get in the way,' said Andrew. 'Yes, that would be it,' said Alex. 'No future for those hats at a party.'

'Do you think Claire has got one of those hats?' said Andrew. 'Wouldn't surprise me,' said Alex. 'She goes in for authenticity these days, Claire does.' 'Usedn't she to?' asked Andrew. He hadn't actually ever known Claire at all well: Claire wasn't from the old crowd; Claire was a *trouvaille* of Alex's own. 'Not as such,' said Alex. 'Not *as such*.'

'And Barbara,' said Andrew, 'does she go in for authenticity?' Alex thought for a moment, or perhaps his mind was merely wandering, under the influence; Andrew waited. Andrew knew the form. 'Very probably,' said Alex at last. 'Shouldn't be at all surprised. Probably where Claire got the idea, come to think of it. Yes, Claire probably caught it from Barbara. Wouldn't surprise me at all.' There was another brief silence. 'She'd look good in one of those hats,' said Andrew. 'I can see her dressed up *à la Bretonne*.' Dressed, undressed, dressed up – Barbara, all golden-brown. '*What?*' said Alex, astounded. '*Claire? À la Bretonne?*' He began to laugh. Poor Claire. Poor Claire, *bien sûr*. 'No, you moron,' said Andrew. 'Barbara, for God's sake.'

'You've got that girl on the brain,' said Alex. Fuck, thought Andrew. The cat's out of the bag, and no mistake. Pretty pussy, nice pussy: come here, puss, nice bag, come on in, puss. He laughed. 'Looks like it,' he said. The dope was wearing off. That was how it seemed to go, these days. It was after three a.m. and he was feeling sober, and very soon he would be abandoned to sadness and solitude and pain once more. 'She's so . . . juicy,' he said. 'Yes,' said Alex. 'She is that. But authentic with it. You want to watch out for these juicy but authentic types. Bad combination, from the masculine point of view.' Andrew looked at him carefully. 'You speak from experience, I take it,' he said. 'Not me,' said Alex. 'No. Just observation. The times we live in. Juice, plus authenticity. There's a lot of it about.'

'Hmmm,' said Andrew. He was thinking, I could just go up there: I can remember the house. The flight of steps, the urns with geraniums, the number: 51. Impossible by public transport. I'll have to buy a car. He was going to buy a car (which heretofore he had told himself he would not need) in order to go and see a woman who had only with difficulty remembered his name. *I hope that she/ Turns out to be/ Someone to watch over me*: because he wanted watching over. Because we all do.

'You must come and see us after Claire gets back,' said Alex. 'Come and have dinner. Meet the brats.' 'I'd love to,' said Andrew. 'Good,' said Alex. 'I'll get Claire to give you a call. I know she'd love to see you again.' 'Any time,' said Andrew. Alex had risen. Andrew got to his feet and saw him out. All the pain, sorrow, failure was over there in the shadows: here under the light was this golden-brown present, this fine, long, delicate filament of future: I'll ring the bank first thing on Monday, he thought; then all I have to do is actually buy the bloody car. How long will that take? I could be behind the wheel by the middle of the week, couldn't I? I could be seeing her before the week is out: couldn't I? *Dear God, could I?*

I could just go up there, thought Alex. Just bloody turn up, unannounced, tomorrow morning. Well, midday. She might just be hungry: she might just be hungry enough to come out for lunch with me. And then . . . can I do this? Should I? No, never mind *should*: fuck *should*. I can, I must, I fucking *will*. *There's a somebody I'm longing to see.* I'll give her *longing to see.* All the way home to Highbury; *longing.* I'll give her *longing.* He noticed the red light coming up only just in time.

There was a message on the answerphone when he got

home. Claire. *I've been trying to get you all evening. I'll try again tomorrow around midday. For God's sake be there.* That was that then. I'll be here. And then there'll be what's left of the afternoon, drifting away into emptiness and waste. No Belsize Park, not tomorrow: not after Claire on the telephone: not, probably, at all. Not ever. Fuck Claire. No: not Claire's fault: sorry, Claire. Poor Claire. *Bien sûr.*

And right now, there's nothing to do but go to bed. Don't drink, don't smoke, and above all don't think. But as Alex drifted towards sleep in the sketchily-made bed he thought, maybe later in the week. Maybe I could manage it later in the week. It was — what? Two years more or less since he'd last seen Barbara; one whole year, one whole year at least since he'd even thought of her. And there, suddenly, she'd been, tonight, as golden as ever. *Longing*, intolerable longing. Then merciful sleep inundated him.

3

'Hello . . .' Andrew's tone was hesitant; he was almost turning away again, as if having after all thought better of the whole enterprise, but he carried on, nevertheless; brave, stalwart. 'Andrew Flynn. I met you the other night at the Carrington party – we came home together with Alex Maclise.' She was still staring at him, quite silent, standing in the doorway. 'Yes,' she said. She had been so sure that she would not see him again. Not that she had particularly wanted to. He was almost turning away again; but he went on.

'Would you like to come out somewhere? We could go and get a Marine Ice, or something. I've just bought this car.' She was suddenly touched. Ice cream. New car. *Sweet.*

'Yes, all right. I'll just – hold on a sec. I'll just get my bag.' And she left him standing there on the threshold. He looked through the open door along a passageway at the end of which was another door through which he could see a tiny kitchen where yet another door, directly opposite this one, but made of glass, gave a view of a trellis covered with creepers beyond which there was evidently a back garden. The doorway on the left of the passage through which she had vanished and through which she now reappeared led presumably to the flat's chief or only room, perhaps a rather large studio room. Would he ever discover the truth?

She came out carrying her large bag and closed the front door behind her. 'Off we go, then,' she said.

After they'd bought the ices he parked the car in a street near Primrose Hill and they walked on the Hill while they finished eating. Then they sat down on the grass. Soon it would be autumn: as the light began to fade, one could already see that haze in the air. They sat quite quiet, each transfixed by the shimmering prospect. That was something he'd forgotten, away there in the USA: the melancholy inhering in the English scene: a heart-rending sense that everything you see before you might in the next instant vanish for ever, that everything trembled on the verge of a sudden and total dissolution.

After some time, unable, unwilling, to keep his own counsel any longer, he spoke. 'This is the first time,' he said slowly, 'since I've been back here, that I've felt really . . .' happy? No: that gave too much away; gave away even more, perhaps, than was the case. 'Yes?' she said. 'Glad,' he said. 'Glad to be back.' She gave him a brief, intelligent stare. 'How long since you came back?' she said. He told her, giving the merest possible account of the circumstances of his solitary return. Then she asked him what he did: I'm a mathematician, he told her. I used to do it; now I mainly teach others to do it. I'm burnt out.

She thought about this for a while. 'Would you like to take me home now?' she said. There was something in her tone: he couldn't, couldn't possibly, believe his luck. 'Yes,' he said. They got up.

She unlocked the front door and he followed her inside, and he saw, now, the mysterious large room. It had French windows at the nether end giving a view of the trellis and glimpses of the garden beyond – chiefly of a large lime tree in the middle distance. 'Sit down,' she said. She went into the kitchen and made some coffee.

Of course it was too good to be true: she couldn't possibly, not possibly, have meant – no; not possibly. Now that he was here, in this room, with the divan bed hugely in view, he couldn't possibly think, couldn't possibly imagine, that she had been inviting him into it. She gave him his coffee and sat down on the edge of the bed. She drank for a while and then leaned back among some cushions. 'Come over here,' she said.

Even before he reached home, he was aching to have her again. His mind felt almost dislocated with happiness; he did not want to think: he was glad to be as incapable as unwilling to do so: he had long ago forgotten what it was to feel this dislocation, this ecstatic dislocation. How soon, how early in the day, could he telephone her? How long would it be before he could be with her again?

4

Barbara let herself into the main house and went into the kitchen with the shopping which she began to unpack and put away where necessary. For most of the day she had been sitting under a tree on Hampstead Heath reading, but it was time to get the dinner ready for her employers, who were two lawyers, and their offspring. She started to clatter about.

Shrieks were now heard from above and footsteps descending the stairs, and two faces appeared around the doorway: two exactly identical androgynous thirteen-year-old faces with floppy fair hair and long eyelashes. 'Hello, Barbara,' they said very politely. 'Can we help you?'

She looked at them. It was easy to do: one could do it indefinitely. There was something almost absurd about their beauty, now on the eve of its perilous transition into the adult form.

'*No*,' she said.

They came into the room. 'We know you don't actually mean that,' said James. 'Of course she doesn't,' said John. 'She needs us much more than we need her.' 'No I don't,' said Barbara. 'I don't need you at all. Now leave me alone.' 'Never,' they said. 'We shall never *ever* leave you.'

'Except when we go away to school,' said John. 'But we're not responsible for that.' They were about to go away to boarding school.

'We could take her with us,' said James. 'No you couldn't,' said Barbara. 'I don't want to go.' 'You'll miss us, you know,' said James. 'You'll simply cry your eyes out,' said John. They started to imitate her imminent grief, crying and wailing and waving their arms in the air in a pantomime of female anguish. Then they suddenly stopped. 'Will you come and see us?' said James. 'Oh, *yeah*,' said John. '*Brilliant.* You can come down on the train and see us. Will you?' 'No,' said Barbara. 'I've got better things to do.' 'I always knew she didn't really care for us,' said James to his brother. 'She has a heart of stone,' said John. 'That's right,' said Barbara. She was getting on with the dinner. 'What are we having?' they asked.

'Smoked salmon,' she said. 'Yuck!' they cried. 'Anything else?' '*Tarte aux asperges*,' she said. '*Ah, ça c'est formidable*,' said James. '*Oui, c'est tout à fait bien*,' said John. 'Anything else?' 'Raspberry fool,' said Barbara. 'Wicked!' they yelled. 'Wic*ed*!' 'Now go away,' she said. 'And let me get on.' 'Couldn't we just watch?' said John. They both sat down at the kitchen table and watched her with their long-lashed blue eyes. She could fairly have eaten them. They would never be like this again: the imminent term would be their first as boarders; they would be changed for ever.

'What did you do today?' she asked. As almost every weekday evening, for the last several months: and then the replies: bizarre accounts of the daily grind at their day school, where the rites designed to prepare them for the approaching initiation were supervised by adults of fabulous eccentricity. That production had now reached its triumphant conclusion; these last weeks of childhood had been allotted to a vacation in France and a flurry of tightly-scheduled activities of the improving kind.

'We've been playing tennis,' said John. 'I won.' 'Actually, it was me,' said James. 'He's lying,' said his brother. 'Now he's told two lies,' said James. They began to fight. 'Okay,' said Barbara. 'Out!' They stopped. 'No, do let us stay,' they pleaded. 'We'll be *so* quiet.' They sat in a dumbshow of utterly inert silence for half a minute and then a faint ringing was heard below. 'Hey, Barbara!' they cried. 'It's your telephone! Shall we go and answer it for you?' '*No*,' she said. 'Leave it.'

'How *can* you?' they yelped. '*Please* let us answer it.' 'No,' she said. 'Anyway, it's stopped.' They were now at last bored with her; John turned to James. 'Shall we go and see if Simon's home?' They got up. 'Goodbye, Barbara darling,' they said. 'Goodbye,' she said. 'Be careful crossing the street.' 'She's pretending that we're babies,' said John. 'It's her way of showing that she really cares about us,' said James. 'She can't help it,' said John, as the front door slammed shut behind them.

5

The meal was almost ready — there were just a few last-minute things left to do. She looked around and began to clear up.

The front door opened and closed again; a single, heavier tread was heard in the hallway. It stopped and then advanced once more towards the kitchen. The master of the house.

'Ah, Barbara.' He stood in the doorway, a much larger and coarser version of his sons, but with dark hair, and enveloped (as one might hope they never should be) in weariness.

'Hello, Tom.'

He looked around at her demesne: he knew perfectly well that he was trespassing. He gestured. 'I — got away early today. Had to pick up the car.' 'Oh, yes.' 'Little blighters about?' 'They've gone to see Simon. So they told me.' 'Ah, yes. Simon. Serena not home yet of course — is she?' 'No, not yet.' 'Well — I might just jump the gun and get myself a g and t. How are we off for tonic — are we okay?' 'Yes, there's plenty; I got some more today. There's some in the fridge. In the door.' 'Oh, yes. Marvellous. You'll join me, won't you?'

Barbara sat down on a chair diagonally opposite to her employer's, shaking her glass gently, watching the bubbles, to all appearances unaware of his scrutiny, with all its helpless hunger. She went on playing, letting him look, letting him hunger. She liked him, but that was as far as it went: that was as far as it *could* go.

'I haven't actually seen you for ages, have I? How have you been keeping? Managing okay down there, are you?' 'Yes, fine, thanks. Everything's fine.' So it was. Now she was looking at him: those eyes. Poor sod. Don't make it worse. Put a stop to it, in fact: enough is enough. 'I'd better get on,' she said. She got up and took the cream from the refrigerator. He didn't ask, like the twins, can I watch you: simply sat, unable to move, watching. She took down a bowl and got the whisk; she poured the cream into the bowl. 'Fool,' she said. 'I'm making a fool.' 'Ah,' he said, cottoning on at last, smiling with relief. For one extraordinary moment he had thought . . . but of course it was so. Yes, he dumbly, helplessly thought, I want her, and I'm a fool to do so, because it's hopeless; entirely out of the question; hopeless. I should go up and change. 'Won't you have another?' he said. She stopped whisking; she smiled. 'No,' she said, 'thank you.' He got another drink and sat down again.

'I can hear your telephone ringing,' he said. 'It's nothing important,' she said, unperturbed. 'Or if it is they'll try again later.' 'Perhaps we should get you an answering machine,' he said very seriously. 'No, really. It's fine as it is.' 'If you're sure.' 'Yes, positive. Thanks all the same.' She was almost done. She finished making the fool and put it in the refrigerator. She put the tart in the oven and set the timer, and wrote a note for Serena to tell her what needed to be told and left it in the agreed place, and he watched her all the while, dumb, helpless. This sort of thing won't actually do, she thought. Still, it hardly ever occurs: if he started to come home early more often then it would really be bad news, but as it is — he'll have forgotten all about me within half an hour.

He's rather a dish, though, she thought! no doubt about that.

6

Alex wandered into Claire's study and stood there, looking around. It was one of the things he sometimes did, when he was alone in the house.

Alex and the house had a whole deep relationship unknown to anyone else. He thought of it, in fact, as in some quasi-spiritual aspect *his* house, his solitary own. It was for one thing his brainwave, the only truly clever thing, he thought, he'd ever done: going in for this big house, back there in the dark ages, in that innocent era before the property boom. The mortgage repayments had become an absolute doddle and the whole heap was now worth several times what it had cost.

But the real beauty of it was that a marriage such as his and Claire's had become was perfectly negotiable: perfectly: as long as one had all this space. All this rare and valuable north London space. And just look at those mouldings, and try those doors: yes, those *are* the original handles. And the skirting – it made up for a lot, an awful lot, that skirting. It made up for vacancy, and ironical courtesy, and alienation, almost. He sometimes wondered if buying this house hadn't been merely clever, but actually prescient.

He always had, of course, a reason for being in Claire's study, a real reason. There was the dictionary, for example. If Claire hadn't been indifferent to his coming in here she wouldn't have insisted on keeping the *Shorter* in here. Alex was damned if he was going to buy another copy just so as to save Claire's feelings. Or his. Claire. Claire's books. He looked, once more, at Claire's books: shelves, positively in the plural shelves, of fiction, virtually all of it contemporary. I never read novels, he said one day. At some point (he hadn't noticed precisely where, along the long slow curve) he had ceased to be a person who read novels; now he too could say, flatly, I never read novels.

No, Claire said, men are always saying that. Well, it's true, he'd said. Yes, of course, said Claire. But the point is the tone of voice: as if you were disclaiming the practice of some solitary vice. Which is what you seem to think novel-reading is. The average man I suppose would rather be caught with his prick in his hand than a novel, God help you all.

And the thing was, he couldn't be bothered arguing: couldn't be bothered pointing out to her that any man so *caught* was up to something one million times more authentic (repeat, authentic) than reading any of the works of . . . and there followed a sample of the names of the novelists reviewed, admired, interviewed and extolled by Claire and her fellows over the past few years: Claire in the broadsheets, Claire across the airwaves, Claire in the glossies, Claire and all her kind: all that avidity, all those queasy phrases: all that crazed enthusiasm: if he'd had the time, if he could have been bothered, he just might have managed to demonstrate, clearly, cleanly, and apocalyptically, that all this activity wasn't, wasn't by any means, wasn't by even half, as harmless as it looked, and that it was in fact the sign, *the very sign* by which one knew, beyond any possible doubt, that civilisation was coming, disgracefully, to its end.

He took down one of Claire's novels, inscribed by the author, and began to read. Yes. You see, he said to himself, as if addressing Claire, as if she might attend to him, as if he might really care that she should, it isn't simply a case of the emperor's having no clothes: the fact is, that *it isn't even the emperor*: it's actually − just take a good look, just open your eyes and for God's sake *look* − it's actually the court bloody eunuch.

He replaced the book, and looked around again, at Claire's desk, at the litter on its surface, the chair (one of her jerseys still draped over its back), the rug beneath it. It was one of the good ones which they'd bought in the early, early days. Caucasian. And at its edge, the daybed. He sat down.

Why did I come in here, he thought. What did I actually come in here *for*. But now at last there was no reason for wondering, none for resisting: now, at last, he gave himself to memory, acute and engulfing. He saw once more (as not, now, for a good twelve months) as in a vivid dream that week (now two years distant) when, on this very daybed, in this very room (not then Claire's study) he had had, for his own, for his very own unforeseen, un-imaginable, incredulous delight, Barbara.

PART II

7

'I *told* you. *Scunthorpe.* Yes, all right, *of course* it's risible, let me know when you've finished laughing and I'll go on, take your time, I wouldn't dream of spoiling your fun.' And she left the room. Alex shook his head – the au pair was clearing away the children's tea, pretending not to notice a thing – and went after her. She was in the sitting-room, lighting a cigarette. She sat down and picked up the *Guardian*.

'Okay, Claire, don't get in a wax with me. You've got to admit – the Scunthorpe Literary Festival – I mean, things have obviously come to a pretty pass when—' and he started to laugh again. She gave him one of her looks, cold, stupefying, and her gaze returned to the newspaper. His laughter drained away. 'Let's take it from the top,' he said, utterly sober, beaten. 'If you're quite ready,' she said. Very cool, very polite: utterly reasonable. 'Yes, absolutely; sock it to me.'

'It's perfectly simple,' she said. 'I'll be in Scunthorpe—' she shot him a look; he did not flinch; not a muscle twitched; he was all attention – 'all next week. Monday to Friday. Coming back Saturday: okay? But that's the week that Astrid will be away – you remember. No, of course you don't. Let that pass. She's going home to Denmark for a week. Her sister's wedding. So I've asked Barbara to come and stay and look after the kids. You can look after yourself. For a week, at any rate.'

'Barbara,' he said.

'Yes, Barbara. *You know, Barbara.*'

'Oh, yes, yes of course. That protégée of yours. Big brown girl, brown eyes?'

'Clever of you to notice. Yes. She'll come over on Sunday night so that I can explain everything: so it *might* be nice if you were around that evening. Do you think you could manage that?' 'Oh, I should think so, yes, why not.' 'Splendid.' There was a pause. Advantage Claire. 'Though I can't *quite* see,' he said, 'what all the fuss is for. Couldn't the children go to your mother's for the week? She loves having them.' 'I wouldn't expect you to have noticed,' said Claire, 'but the fact is, they've both started school. And at the moment, as it happens, the schools are not on holiday.' 'Ah,' he said. 'Of course. School. Still, at their ages—' 'A week is in fact absolutely crucial,' said Claire. She was still cool, still polite, still reasonable. He was beaten. 'Whatever you say,' he said. 'So this Barbara – I mean – knows what she's doing, does she? Understands kids?'

Claire looked at him, and then began to laugh: long peals of genuine laughter. 'You really are priceless,' she said, and laughed some more. But at last she stopped, and in the aftermath her face looked for an instant appallingly sad. 'Oh, God,' she said. 'Oh, God.'

He ought to have gone to her and put his arms around her, but he couldn't: it wasn't simply that he didn't want to: *he couldn't.*

He couldn't make it better, but he didn't make it worse. 'Drink?' he said. 'Yes, why not,' said Claire. 'Mine's a spritzer.' 'Right you are,' he said, and he got up and went into the kitchen.

And that was how Barbara came to be staying in the house, in his house, for virtually a whole week, two years ago; because of the Scunthorpe Literary Festival. Well done, Scunthorpe. And Astrid's sister's wedding. Three cheers for Astrid's sister. That was how Barbara came to be sleeping, for six nights, on this very daybed, in this very room. It had been the spare room in those days, when what was now the spare room had been the au pair's room. The spare room . . . a phrase to conjure with: a space to conjure with: what say you, M. Bachelard?

8

Marguerite was eight and Percy was six. Percy was having a hard time getting out from under Marguerite, but he was getting there. Meanwhile, he had quite a lot to put up with: Barbara couldn't help wondering whether Marguerite couldn't have handled the whole situation by herself: clean clothes, journeys to and from school, food on the table, bath and bedtime at nine p.m. sharp, the lot, Percy stumbling along in her grasp.

As it was: How was school today, Marguerite? *Infantile.* Percy? *Infantile.* He's just saying that, he doesn't really know what it means. Yes I do! *What* does it mean? *I'm* not going to tell you. Go and find out for yourself!

Barbara wasn't sure what, if anything, she ought to do about Alex's supper: she ate with the children. The first night she made cauliflower cheese, enough for four, and put some aside. Alex got home every evening in time to see the children for an hour or so between bath and bedtime. After they were safely put away for the night he came awkwardly into the kitchen where Barbara was sitting listening to Radio 4, feeling strange and homesick. She looked up and turned off the wireless. 'Oh, please—' said Alex. 'No, it's all right,' said Barbara. 'I wasn't really listening.'

'Would you like a drink?' said Alex. Lord: was he going to have to socialise with this stranger in the house every evening until Claire's return? 'Oh –' said Barbara, as unequal, now that she was in its midst, to the situation as he, 'only if——' and she broke off. What was she meant to do? Alex was so foreign, dark, remote and unpeaceful. Every strange man is Mr Rochester, she thought, almost laughing. She smiled to herself. Alex, seeing this, smiled back. 'Go on,' he said, 'be a devil.' She laughed. He took a bottle of white wine out of the refrigerator. 'This do?' he asked. 'Yes,' she said. He put it on the table and fetched two glasses and sat down. Then he poured it out, rather ceremoniously. He held up his own glass. '*A vos beaux yeux*,' he said. There was only the smallest hint, the palest and most ghostly hint, of irony in his tone. What a horrible man, thought Barbara. What a nasty Mr Rochester it is. She smiled again. Why is she always smiling, Alex thought vaguely. He frowned and looked around the room.

'By the way,' he said, 'do help yourself to anything while you're here, of course – anything you fancy. Drink in that cupboard, more wine under the stairs, food – you know where that is – did Claire leave you some money for shopping if you need anything? Good, let me know if you run out. Anything else you need? You know how everything works, don't you – yes – know where everything is? Know how the video works and so on? Well, Percy can work that for you. Or Marguerite. How were they today? Yes, they seem perfectly happy. Well, this is terribly good of you, really.'

'Not at all,' said Barbara. 'It's a pleasure.' 'Good,' said Alex. 'Good.' Barbara got up. 'I wasn't sure what you might want to do about dinner,' she said. 'With Claire not here. I ate with the children. But I kept you some of this in case. Cauliflower cheese. It just needs heating up.' 'Oh,' he said. 'I say, that's very thoughtful of you.' 'It's nothing,' said Barbara. 'Shall I put it in the oven for you now?' 'Well, I suppose,' said Alex. 'Why not. Thank you.' 'Give it about twenty minutes,' said Barbara. 'And thank you for the drink. I think I'll go upstairs now and read for a while.' She was achingly homesick. Now that the children were lost to sleep and Claire altogether absent she felt merely strange and unhappy here. I hate it here, she thought. I hate this house.

She put her head politely around the door to the sitting-room before she went to bed. 'I just came to say good night,' she said. 'Oh, right, yes,' said Alex. 'Good night. And thank you for everything.' 'Good night,' said Barbara. And retreated. Alex switched on the telly and watched *Newsnight*. When it was over he switched it off quickly in order to avoid the *Late Show* title sequence. That howling fucking wolf, he thought; says it all. He sat staring at the blank screen for a long, long time. She's beautiful, he thought. I hadn't noticed before: she's beautiful. Extraordinary to think that this beautiful girl was here, in his house, sleeping under his roof, looking after his children: completely extraordinary: what a rum do, he thought. And then he went to bed.

9

'We had bangers tonight,' said Barbara. 'There are still some left, shall I cook them for you?' 'Oh, you mustn't bother about me,' said Alex, 'really. I can manage for myself. You've done quite enough already.' 'It's nothing,' said Barbara. This was the Tuesday night. 'Look,' she said, turning on the grill. 'I'll put them on for you, and you can turn them and finish them off.' 'Fine,' said Alex. 'Right.' 'And there's potato salad in the fridge,' said Barbara, 'if you fancy it.' 'Oh, good,' said Alex. 'Et cetera,' said Barbara. 'Yes, fine,' said Alex. 'So,' she said, 'I'll leave you in peace—' 'Listen,' said Alex, 'do stay down here and watch television if you like, or whatever – you won't be disturbing me.'

'No, really,' said Barbara. 'I'd really rather read.' 'Well, if you'd rather,' said Alex. 'But please don't feel—' 'No,' said Barbara. 'Please don't worry. I'm fine, truly.' 'Yes, well,' said Alex. 'I'll see you later,' said Barbara. She came to say good night as she had the night before; he watched *Newsnight* again and turned off the howling fucking wolf again; and he stared at the blank screen again, and thought about how beautiful she was, how beautiful.

On Wednesday night there was lasagne. 'There's plenty left over,' she said. 'Shall I put it in the oven for you?' 'Yes,' he said. 'That would be kind.' When she had closed the oven door she stood there, hesitant. 'Would you mind if I joined you to watch the *Late Show* tonight,' she said. 'I'd hate to miss Claire's thing.' 'Oh!' he said, taken by surprise. 'By all means, no, watch by all means – anything you like. *Claire's* thing? I hadn't actually realised—' 'Scunthorpe,' she said. 'There's an item tonight about the Scunthorpe Festival.' 'Oh, of course,' said Alex, not batting an eyelid. 'Scunthorpe. Must watch that.' 'Well, I'll see you later,' said Barbara. 'Yes, whenever you like,' said Alex. 'Come early and catch *Newsnight*. Make a night of it.' 'Yes, I'll see,' said Barbara. Nasty Mr Rochester.

He writhed inwardly throughout Claire's Scunthorpe piece. Fifteen minutes seemed an era. It was, by chance, the concluding item; he switched off the set – 'unless there's something else –?' 'No, not at all, do switch off' – and sat down again. Barbara got up. 'That was nice,' she said. 'Yes,' he said, still writhing. 'Nice.' 'Well—' she said. I want her, he thought. *I want her.* He felt that if this was wanting, he had never wanted before. 'I say,' he said, 'I wondered – shall I bring something back for supper tomorrow night? I can get home in time for the kids' tea if I step on it. Do you like fish and chips? There's rather a good place nearby. The brats are mad about fish and chips, the brats are.' 'Yes,' said Barbara. 'That would be terrific, actually. Thank you.' 'It's no trouble,' said Alex.

10

The day had been warm, an echo of the summer just gone, and the evening was still mild; at Percy's brilliant suggestion they ate the fish and chips in the garden. He and Marguerite ran back and forth with glasses and napkins and plates. 'Is this a party?' asked Percy. 'Is this a party?'

Afterwards Alex played *pétanque* with the children. When they were in their baths he came downstairs again and into the kitchen. Barbara was sitting at the table writing. She looked up. 'I'm just making a shopping list,' she told him, as if she thought it necessary to explain her presence there. 'I have to get a few things – I promised the children we'd make a cake tomorrow after school. For Claire. To welcome her back. I just have to get a few things—' 'Oh, yes, right,' said Alex. 'Carry on. Are you sure you don't mind? It's awfully good of you. Well beyond the call of duty.' 'No, it's nothing,' said Barbara. 'I want to.'

'Chocolate cake,' said Alex, flatly. He spoke almost as if prompted from Beyond. Barbara stared at him. 'Yes,' she said. 'How did you know?' Their identities seemed to have merged in a moment of almost sickeningly intense communion; and then reason suddenly returned. 'Oh, of course – the children must have told you,' she said.

'No,' he replied. His face was grave; almost sad. 'No,' he said; 'as a matter of fact, they didn't. Didn't mention it at all. Can't think where I got the idea.' 'Oh, well,' said Barbara; 'I suppose, after all, it's most people's first choice.' 'Yes, probably,' said Alex. That moment of terrible communion was far behind them. 'Have a drink?' he said. 'I'll just look at the children first,' said Barbara.

She came back after a while. 'They're ready to be kissed good night,' she told him. He went upstairs and she poured herself a glass of wine. She was sipping at it when he returned; she was thinking, only two more nights, and this one's half done, only two more nights, thank God.

'Let's go into the sitting-room,' he said. 'Unless you've anything else planned for the evening?' 'No,' she said, 'as it happens I haven't.'

They sat on the sofa opposite the blank television screen. 'Anything you fancy watching?' said Alex. 'You only have to say.' 'No, really,' said Barbara. 'But don't let me stop you—' 'No,' said Alex. 'I – won't you have some more?' He picked up the wine bottle. I'll have another glass, thought Barbara, to show willing, and then I can escape.

'I don't quite remember,' said Alex, 'how it is that you and Claire seem to know each other – you're not in her line of work, are you?' God forbid, God forbid. Wait for it now. 'No,' said Barbara. 'We met at the yoga class.'

Oh, God, but you do take the biscuit: every single time: yoga! Come back the contemporary novel, all is forgiven! 'Yoga?' said Alex. 'I didn't know Claire did *yoga*. Whatever next?'

'Well,' said Barbara, 'I don't know if she does still. But she did.' 'Good God,' said Alex. 'When was that?' 'Well, about a year ago,' said Barbara. 'Yes, just a year. I was living in Islington then and there was a yoga class at the adult education place. Tuesday mornings. And we met there.

And we just, you know, got to know each other. I used to come back here for lunch sometimes afterwards. Sometimes I went with Claire to fetch the children from school – I was still here once or twice when you got back from work.' She paused, but Alex said nothing. 'And I came to babysit one evening because it was one of Astrid's evenings off.' She paused again. 'That was when you were in Belfast,' she said shyly. 'Oh, yes,' said Alex. 'When I was in Belfast. Dangerman.' 'Yes,' said Barbara. And suddenly she was almost overwhelmed by the desire to turn to him, to put her arms around him: suddenly she wanted to be next to him, to feel all his warmth. God, what on earth had possessed her? She must be sloshed: how utterly absurd!

'So that's how I more or less got to know the children,' she said. Her voice sounded weak and distant to her ear. 'So—' 'Yes, I see,' said Alex. 'Well, they've fallen on their feet, I must say.' 'How do you mean?' 'I mean, jolly nice for them to have you running around after them and so forth. Cakes and whatnot. It really is exceedingly good of you. I'm very seriously obliged to you.'

'But they're sweeties,' said Barbara. 'It's a pleasure.' 'Oh, do you really think so?' He seemed genuinely pleased by the compliment. 'Yes, of course. Don't you?' He laughed. 'I'm prejudiced,' he said. She thought for a moment. 'Percy had some homework today,' she said. 'Oh, yes,' said Alex rather vaguely. He was pouring himself another glass; 'Yes, that school of theirs is very progressive. Infant noses to the grindstone.' 'He managed to do it all by himself,' she said. 'Oh, yes? Jolly good. My God, I should bloody hope so, though. Don't want him slacking off at this stage.' She laughed. There was a pause. He picked up the bottle again and looked at her enquiringly; she shook her head.

'I think –' she began to stir; 'I think I might turn in actually. There's a book I want to finish—' 'Oh, of course, I'm keeping you—' *as a matter of fact I wish to God I were.* He got up. 'Well – I'll see you in the morning, then. Sleep well!' She said good night and was gone; he sat down once more and stared after her. I haven't a clue, he thought, I haven't a fucking clue. I shouldn't even be thinking of it. And yet he could think of absolutely nothing else.

II

'Oh, by the way,' he said as he was leaving the next morning for work, 'don't worry about my supper tonight, not that you should do anyway, but I'll be back late – Friday night I usually meet people and so on. The kids know the routine, don't you, kids. No dinosaur tonight. See you both in the morning. Be good or I'll have you for breakfast tomorrow morning, okay?' He bent and kissed them both and straightened up.

Their eyes met for an instant. 'I'll see you later,' he said. 'If you're still up – leave all the lights on if you go up before I get in. Right, off we go – oh! one thing – this is one of Mrs Brick's days, isn't it? Could you make sure she does some ironing, I'm down to my last shirt.' 'Yes,' said Barbara, 'I'll make sure.' 'Jolly good,' he said. 'Thanks. Bye now.' And he was gone. Barbara felt strangely, unaccountably, deserted.

'If you could find time to iron Mr Rochester's shirts,' she said to Mrs Brick, 'it would be such a help.' 'Mr Rochester?' said Mrs Brick. 'Oh, God,' said Barbara. 'I must be dreaming. Sorry. I mean Mr Maclise of course. Goodness!' 'It's those kiddies addling your brains,' said Mrs Brick. 'Kiddies do that to you. You wait until you have your own. Mr Rochester's the least of it.' 'Yes, I suppose so,' said Barbara weakly. 'So if you'll be all right here for the time being, Mrs Brick, I think I'll go for a walk.'

She covered the whole of Highbury, thinking of Mr Rochester, thinking of Mr Maclise. Alex. And I am not sloshed now, she thought. *Nor was I last night. Alex.*

Alex let himself in. The house was silent, shining. He knew he should not find her in the sitting-room: it was too much to hope for. No: silent, bare. He turned and went up the stairs.

One thing about these splendid doors, with their original handles, was that they had shrunk ever so slightly from their frames: a filament of bright light could just be discerned along the edges of the door to the spare room. He knocked very gently and entered.

Barbara looked up, astonished. She was sitting hunched up on the bed, fully clothed, reading. 'Hello,' he said. 'Do you mind – I just wanted to see you for a moment. I've brought you something.'

She put down the book and sat up, astounded and speechless, and he handed her a smallish carrier bag. 'It's just a present,' he said. 'To thank you for looking after the brats.' 'Oh, but you shouldn't have done that,' she said. 'There really was no need.' She was deeply taken aback; she was almost alarmed. He shrugged. 'It's nothing much,' he said. 'Open it and see.' He sat down: he was weak at the knees, almost trembling. 'Do you mind if I sit down,' he muttered. She edged slightly further away from him. 'No, please,' she said.

She looked dazedly into the carrier bag and withdrew a flat parcel which she unwrapped, breaking a gold foil seal in order to do so. 'What a lovely parcel,' she said. 'It's a pity to open it.' The paper was thick and shiny, with tiny gold stars on an ivory-coloured ground. Inside the wrapping was a flat wooden box with French writing in a rococo copperplate hand on its lid, which she at last opened. There lay revealed twelve marrons glacés. 'Oh!' she exclaimed. She stared at the spectacle, bewitched.

'I hope I didn't make a mistake,' he said. 'I thought and thought. But chocolates seemed so banal, in comparison. Of course, if you don't like marrons glacés, well – well, it's a pretty good joke!' He laughed. 'I'm sorry to spoil a joke,' she said, 'but I'm bound to say that I simply adore them.' They both laughed. 'Thank you so much,' she said. She was still astounded to find him in here, amazed by what he had done, and still, at the end of this whole day, bewildered and also appalled by the sensations he had begun to arouse in her: so bewildered, so appalled, that she had not seen the poetic inevitability of this development. Suddenly she saw it now. What an idiot I am, she thought: of course I must by this have begun to *care* for Mr Rochester. Her heart began terribly to beat: whatever had possessed her last night possessed her now completely.

'Won't you have one?' she asked him, offering the box. 'Will you?' he said. 'Yes,' she replied, 'of course.' 'Then I will too,' he said, and he took one. They were much closer to each other than ever heretofore, he on the edge of the bed – it was the daybed, this daybed, it was rather hard – she leaning up against the wall, the lamplight behind her. 'Luscious,' she said, eating.

'This bed is really rather hard, isn't it?' he said. 'I hope you haven't been sleeping badly.' 'No, of course not,' she said. 'It's fine.' She looked at him; their eyes met. He was lost; willingly lost. It was all wrong, but it was the only right, the only possible, thing in all the universe. 'I've fallen in love with you,' he said. 'I want you so badly I can't think straight.'

Tears sprang into her eyes. She was overwhelmed: 'You know it's no good,' she said. '*Claire.*'

'Oh, Claire,' he said. 'Don't you know about me and Claire?' She didn't say anything; he looked at her and saw the tears in her eyes. 'We don't sleep together,' he said. 'If you'll allow the euphemism. Not since Percy was a toddler. We've been finished for years, Claire and I. We just have a *modus operandi*.' 'I'm sorry,' she said. He looked at her again. 'Forget about that,' he said. He took her hand and kissed the palm, then the wrist, then her mouth; they lay down together on the daybed, this daybed: it was rather hard: he started to kiss her again – he was still holding her hand: and it all began. It took aeons upon aeons, vast tracts of spangled time: worlds were born and died, planets described their courses around indescribable stars; they drifted and soared through another, occult universe contingent on this one (or is this one on that?) – having by grace escaped, or been freed, from the tyranny of language.

12

'I'll see to the kids in the morning,' he murmured as he left her. The morning was breaking as he spoke. He kissed her damp hair. 'Sleep as late as you want.' She came down just after nine o'clock: Alex was in the garden with the children playing shuttlecock. He saw her through the window and came inside.

'I usually take them to Victoria Park on Saturday mornings,' he said. 'And then I give them lunch in a caff. Will you come with us?' She almost quailed before the intensity of his gaze. 'No – I'll stay here,' she said; 'I'll ice the cake.' He looked out of the window. The children were playing frantically against each other now instead of together against him. He watched them as he spoke.

'Claire should get here around three,' he said. 'As soon as you like after that I'll take you home. Just say when you're ready.' 'Thank you,' she said. 'No, you don't understand,' he said. 'I'm sorry,' she said. 'What don't I understand?' He almost wanted to hit her. He took her hand and held it very tightly. 'I'm not doing you a favour,' he said. 'Nothing now that I can ever do for you, or with you, or to you, or – any preposition you like – could be a favour. You must never say thank you to me, never again, *never*.' Tears came into her eyes. 'Don't cry,' he said, 'don't.' She bit her lips. 'I'm going to make some coffee,' she said; he let go her hand and she went to fetch the kettle. 'Do you want some?' 'No,' he said. 'It's time we went.'

He opened the window and called the children and sent them upstairs for their jackets. 'We'll be back here some time after lunch, then,' he said. 'Two–ish, I suppose. Is there anything you want brought back from the shops, or anything?' She shook her head. The children were at the front door, waiting for him. They began to call. 'Daddy! Daddy! Alex! A-a-le-ex!' He turned and went. She stood at the kitchen doorway and waved them all goodbye, and then she sat down at the kitchen table, waiting for the coffee to finish filtering. She crossed her arms on the table and leaned her head on them, succumbing to the state of ecstasy into which she had been cast, as into an abyss.

13

She wrapped the box of marrons glacés in its original paper once more; she wrapped the carrier bag around the reconstituted package and placed the whole parcel at the bottom of her travelling bag. Then she packed all her clothes on top, and squashed down the sides all the incidentals, thinking carefully, forgetting nothing. She saw to the used linen: to everything: that there should be no trace of her occupation of this room, with its square window overlooking a hawthorn tree. She would never, she knew, enter it again, and she stood silent for several minutes, wishing it farewell. She ached to be gone from this house.

'The children have something for you,' said Alex. They were looking hugely self-conscious and self-important, and Percy had charge of a large awkward parcel, which he handed to her. 'For me? How lovely. But why?' 'It's to thank you,' said Marguerite, with almost adult fluency, 'for looking after us.' 'Yes,' said Percy, 'it's to thank you. To *thank* you.' 'How very sweet of you,' she said. She wanted to cry again: she saw, with anguish, how much she would miss them.

She began to open the parcel, which for its size was disconcertingly light, and found a very large natural sponge, about the size of a football. She exclaimed with genuine delight: it was a thing she had long coveted. 'It's perfect,' she said. She turned it around in her hands, looking at all its beautiful irregular surfaces. 'I chose it!' cried Percy. 'Clever Percy,' said Barbara. 'Thank you.' 'That's all right,' said Percy.

Alex was standing behind the children, watching her. 'I chose you something too,' said Marguerite in a smallish voice. 'But it's not the main thing,' said Percy. 'The sponge is the *main* thing. This is only something extra.' Barbara glanced quickly at his sister and they exchanged a brief and knowing look, and Marguerite handed her a very small package. 'It's to go with the sponge,' she explained. Barbara opened it: a cake of pink soap in the shape of a rabbit. 'It's adorable,' she said. 'Smell it,' said Marguerite. 'It smells of roses.' It did, too. 'You're beautiful,' said Barbara. 'Both of you. Come and let me kiss you.' She hugged them to her, one each side, and then quickly let them go. 'Now who wants to decorate the cake,' she said.

She put it, lavishly covered in chocolate icing, on the table and set them to placing a quantity of coloured sugar flowers over its surface as they would, and went upstairs to fetch her bag. Claire must soon return; she must then linger as long as politeness required and then, at last – then – outside a taxi was heard; the slamming of its door; the front door opening, and a cry: Claire.

She waited until the noise of the children's reunion with their mother had subsided a little and then she came downstairs, and the charade began. It involved tea, cake, stories, news, jokes, commendations, reminders, pro-testations of gratitude and of pleasure, and promises of an early meeting, but it was done at last, Alex hovering terribly in the background. Barbara glanced at him: 'Ready?' he said. Claire looked up at them. 'I'll just run

Barbara home,' he said. As they were leaving the room he turned back for a moment. 'I might just call in on Giles on the way back,' he said, 'unless you need me here for anything?' 'No,' said Claire, 'call in on Giles by all means. I don't need you.' She turned back to the children and Alex and Barbara left the house.

14

'I don't even know where you live,' said Alex. She told him and he turned on the ignition. He had not touched her. They might have been virtual strangers: they might be. They drove westwards in silence.

At the top of the house, she unlocked a door and they entered her room. It was the smaller, back, room of the two on this floor; she crossed it and opened the window. He followed her and stood behind her, looking out at the Camden Town roofscape. 'I'll just make sure the plants are all right,' she said. In one corner there was an unaccountable butler's sink, full of pot plants. She examined them and turned around. 'They're all right,' she said. 'They haven't dried out. I left them plenty of water, I hoped they'd be all right. Would you like some tea?'

'Shut up,' he said. 'Leave all that alone.' He looked around quickly, judging the distance to the bed, which was in the opposite corner, adjacent to the window; he seized her by the hand and pulled her towards him. He kissed her mouth for a moment and then he pushed her on to the bed and flung himself down upon her: *now I know what hell is like*, he said: *what do you mean*, she said: *the whole afternoon*, he said, *seeing you and not having you: the whole afternoon, until now.*

But he didn't know precisely what he was talking about: he had not been in hell, only in one of its more salubrious suburbs. He was none the less in a place he might call heaven now; as was she: heaven, or one of its more salubrious suburbs.

'Claire usually takes the children down to Surrey on Sundays,' said Alex. 'To see her parents.' 'I see,' said Barbara. 'So—' said Alex. He turned his head and looked at her. 'Shall I come back tomorrow, then,' he said. 'Or shall I shoot myself?' 'Come back here first, at any rate,' said Barbara. 'All right,' said Alex. 'About midday.' 'Yes,' said Barbara. He made love to her again (falling, flying) and then he left.

15

She led the way up the uncarpeted stairs (the windows on the landings had panes of coloured glass around their margins) and they entered the room once more. He seized her around the waist and began to kiss her: they had exchanged barely a word. He went on kissing her, as if he had been starving. He had, indeed, been starving. They lay down, and it all began again. Alex had been starving for years, years, years. 'It's nice like this,' he whispered to her once; '*it's so nice like this.*' 'Yes,' she said. 'Everything with you is nice.'

All that time later, he said 'Are you hungry? Shall we go somewhere and have some lunch?' They found a Middle Eastern place, almost empty because it was so long past lunch time, and ate some little pies filled with cream cheese and spinach. They had pistachio ices and coffee and smoked *beedies*. 'I got these on the way,' said Alex, looking pleased with himself.

'I wanted to bring you some flowers,' he said, 'but there were none of the right kind. I drove around for ages looking for some but all I saw were frightful carnations and chrysanthemums and so I had to give it up. I feel mortified.' He laughed. 'When I think of all the wonderful flower shops I've passed,' he said, 'when there was no one to buy them for.' 'It's Sunday after all,' Barbara said. 'Yes,' said Alex. 'If this were France, now. Shall we go there?'

'Alex,' she said; it was still strange saying his name, now: his sacred, sacred name; he looked at her. 'Alex,' she said, looking at him seriously, 'what are we going to do?' 'Go back to your place, don't you think?' he said. He was looking at her as seriously as she at him. She said nothing and he stroked her thigh under the table. 'Let's go,' he murmured. He leaned over and whispered something in her ear, and she smiled and pushed back her chair and got up. He rose and looked at the bill and put some notes with it on the table and they left.

He held her hand very tightly all the way home. 'I'm afraid you'll fly away,' he said, 'and I'll never get you back. Like a helium balloon.' She laughed. He went on holding her hand all the way up the stairs and as they entered the room; he leaned against the door and pulled her towards him, still holding her hand. 'Take off your clothes,' he said. 'I can't with one hand,' she protested. 'Go on,' he said, 'just *do* it.' She began to unbutton her blouse with one hand. He started to help her undress, with his free hand. It all took quite a long time: 'I hope you're enjoying this,' he said, kissing her mouth, 'as much as I am.' Then he began to undress. She lay on the bed, watching him. It all took a long, long time.

'I know what it means, now,' he said, almost wonderingly, almost to himself – 'What?' she said. 'With my body I thee worship,' he said. 'What is it?' she said. 'Is it from a poem?' 'No,' he said, slowly. 'It's from the marriage service. "The Solemnization of Matrimony". In the Book of Common Prayer.' 'Oh,' she said. 'The old prayer book.' 'Yes,' he said. 'The old prayer book. *The* Prayer Book. I suppose you're too young to have known it.'

'I didn't know you went in for that sort of thing,' she said. 'God, and so on.' 'I don't,' he said. 'But with my body

I thee worship. I know what it means, now.' He half sat up; he wanted to go on. '*I know what it means*. Do you see? It's the most astounding thing. Just think about it. I mean, I thought – you know, at school we used to read the Prayer Book, the Book of Common Prayer, surreptitiously during sermons.' He laughed. 'One got to know it pretty well, God knows how they get through the time now. I suppose they have to listen to the sermons, poor blighters. *With my body I thee worship*. I suppose I was about fourteen when I first came across that. I wondered how it could be true. I thought it was just some sort of metaphor. And now I know what it means. After almost twenty-five years.' He laughed again. 'To think,' he said, 'that the best, the truest, most literal description of sex that we have in the language is from the hand of some Tudor clergyman. Cranmer, I suppose. Well, who better, after all. But still.'

'*Now* do you believe in God?' she said. He laughed. 'No,' he said; 'only that Mary is His mother.' He was suddenly serious again: he looked down at her. 'Stay quite still,' he said, 'while I thee worship.' She did as he had asked for as long as she possibly could.

16

It was afterwards again; the light was fading. She sat by the window in a red dressing-gown. She had made some tea. Alex was dressed again, because soon he would have to go.

'Alex,' she said, 'what are we going to do?'

'How do you mean?' he said.

'I mean,' she said, '*what are we going to do?*'

He looked at her for a while. 'Come over here for a moment,' he said. 'No.' 'Yes, just for a moment. I have to talk to you. I can't do it while you're over there.' She came reluctantly and he pulled her down beside him and put his arms around her. They were lying back across the bed and he kissed her cheek. 'Don't you really understand,' he said, 'what we're going to do?'

'You'd better tell me,' she said. 'I'm not sure that I do.'

He was silent for some time, holding her in his arms. 'I meant it quite literally when I said, with my body I thee worship. I was absolutely serious. I am still.' He paused. He was having to articulate what was too new and too rare and too strange to articulate. 'I feel . . . stunned. As you see, this is a new experience for me. In fact I feel as if I know something that no one else does. Except perhaps that Tudor clergyman. I've hardly begun to take it in, I'm too amazed by it to be able to think about it.'

They were both silent for a time. They were both still, after all, in a state of amazement.

Then there was a change in the temperature and he spoke almost abruptly. 'But as you see, otherwise,' he said, 'I'm in it up to the neck.' She thought about this for a moment but her head began to swim. 'I'm not sure—' she began, slowly; he cut her off. There was only the faintest vibration of irritation in his voice: only she would have perceived it; it lacerated her heart. 'I have obligations,' he said. 'You've known that from the beginning. You know my situation as well as I do. Do we really need to discuss it? I have a wife and two children and a household to maintain: those are the givens.'

She thought for a moment, but a piece of iron had been driven suddenly into her soul. 'You mean,' she said, '*you mean*—'

'I mean,' he said, 'and perhaps I should have said this clearly at the start, but it never occurred to me that it could be necessary, that I can't think of leaving Claire and the children: surely you see that. This has nothing to do with how things stand between me and Claire – well, maybe it does. I mean, we have, as I said, a *modus operandi*. Of which the object is to raise Marguerite and Percy as peacefully and as properly as we humanly can. I couldn't even think of breaking up the family until at the earliest Percy is settled in at Westminster. Assuming he gets in. And that's seven years off. What else did you expect?'

'I thought,' she said, 'I thought—' and she could not now, did not dare, now, say what she had thought, so wrongly thought; she could not go on, now, because she saw that she was coming – no, had come – to something dreadful. 'You thought, I suppose,' he said, 'that we would run away together and live happily ever after, did you?' 'Yes,' she said.

He was silent for a long time, holding her in his arms, stroking her hair. 'Haven't we run away together,' he said sadly. 'Shan't we live happily ever after?'

'But we won't be together,' she said. 'I thought we'd be *together*.' 'But we *are*,' he said. 'We won't be,' she said. 'Very soon, we won't be. You'll be at home and I shall be here. And then – how often shall we be able to meet after that? No, don't tell me. I know. But even that is not really the point. We'll be sneaking about behind Claire's back, deceiving her and the children, behaving as if this were something disgraceful, secret – *it just won't do. I can't do it. Don't you see?'* And she had pulled away from him, she was sitting up and looking at him, and he knew she was right. He knew, with the coldest and most terrible dread and certainty, that she was right.

'But we must,' he said. 'It's all we have.'

17

It was as if his utterance had come from far away, from some never-before-revealed chamber of his mind, and it echoed down long corridors into a corresponding, equally remote chamber of hers: they sat, marvelling at and almost petrified by these echoes. She made a terrible effort. 'It isn't enough,' she said. 'It is not *it*.' And he saw that she was right: of course, she was right.

'Of course, Claire can look after herself,' he said, slowly; 'my absence would be neither here nor there as far as Claire is concerned, as long as everything kept ticking over; but Percy – Marguerite – you couldn't possibly think, you couldn't *possibly* have thought that there was any question of my disturbing their lives in this way, could you? The house would have to go, for a start – I couldn't run that plus another household somewhere else, as matters stand: their lives would be very seriously altered – you couldn't really have thought I'd do that to them?'

And he began, wonderingly, to face the possibility, the terrible possibility, that she really had. She was silent, she too having been made to see a different conformation from the one she had taken unreflectingly for granted. It was some time before she was able to answer him.

'Other people seem to separate,' she said in a small voice. 'Other families break up, and everyone seems to manage. Oh, of course I know there are wretched divorces where

the children are damaged and never readjust, but I thought
– since you and Claire – I thought – perhaps,' she said, in
an even smaller voice, 'perhaps Marguerite and Percy
would be happier if you and Claire were no longer
together. Since you don't love each other.'

'Claire and I don't quarrel,' he said sharply. 'We may not
be a loving or even affectionate couple but we've always
treated each other politely in front of the children at least.
They accept us as we are.'

'Yes, yes,' she said, desperately. 'I'm sorry, I'm sorry – I
didn't mean to imply – I just thought – I—' and she
began, quietly, helplessly, to weep. Her tears were appalling.
He rocked her in his arms. 'You're so much younger than
I am,' he said. 'I was forgetting. You must be, I suppose,
ten years younger: you couldn't have known what one
knows another ten years down the road. You see what
having children does to one!' And for a time he thought,
quite irrationally, and in a kind of desperation, that, now
that she had seen what he had always seen, her terrible
declaration, It is not *it*, might be nullified, and that she
would no longer be right in so saying, and that he would
no longer see her to be.

Her tears had ceased; she seemed quite calm and lay
very still in his arms. They were both silent for some time
and then he began to speak, hesitantly, almost reluctantly.
'There is nothing I can say to you,' he said; 'there are no
words, except that clergyman's, that describe what I feel,
and even those are not quite the whole of it. I can't tell
you anything, and as you see I can't promise you anything,
or even offer you anything, except myself; whatever that
should mean. And for what it may be worth.'

There was another silence; the room had grown quite
dark. He could sense that she was reflecting on everything

that he had said, and done, and been, and he waited in fear for what she would say. Her voice when eventually she spoke was quite clear and level; she might have been talking to Percy.

'It won't do,' she said. 'We can't – go on.' She paused. 'I don't know whether it would be different if I didn't know Claire, and the children, but as it is – it isn't possible. It isn't worthy of us.' Of course she was right; he knew she was right. 'We won't see each other again,' she said, and she held his hand very tightly, showing that she was his own: that she belonged to him, with all her being.

18

'This has nothing, absolutely nothing, to do with Claire or the children,' he said. 'This – this – there is no word for our situation, yours and mine: this *place* we've come to is ours alone, it has *nothing to do* with anything else in the world or in our lives, it's ours alone. You can't possibly mean what you've said, you can't possibly be saying that this *place* doesn't exist. After the time we've spent here.'

'It exists,' she said. 'But we can't go on being in it.'

'*Why not*,' he said. She went on as if talking to Percy in one of his moods of deliberate recalcitrance. 'It's not separate from the rest of our lives, or the rest of our selves, or the rest of the world,' she said. 'It only *feels* as if it is. *That's the whole point of it.* Don't you see?'

He was silent, frozen with dread: he had seen that she was right, he had hoped to dissuade her (and himself) nevertheless, but he had never truly, never to the depths of his being, believed that they would really act upon the principles which she had enunciated. He had never until now thought seriously that he might not see her again.

'You see,' she said, 'I shouldn't be able ever again to see Claire, or the children; not as your secret lover. I couldn't do it, you know that I couldn't. It would be unimaginably – what is the word? Something even worse than deceitful. And then simply to stop seeing them, in that situation, would be just as bad. You do see what I mean, don't you?'

Of course he did. Unimaginably deceitful, unimaginably tasteless; either way: unimaginable.

'As it is,' she smiled to herself ruefully, 'I shall have to find a tactful way of not seeing them again, anyway.' And he saw that this too was the case. She would not see any of them again, at any rate for some long time. Tactfully, apparently by accident, she would withdraw.

And he realised now, as had she from the start, that the moral argument was always inexorable, that it over-whelmed even the enchantment which had befallen them both: still half within their secret, sacred place they looked out together on a terrible world which the exercise of virtue alone could make tolerable. It was possible to see and comprehend and even accept this now, when they were sated; the anguish they felt was all in their minds; in the days, the weeks, the months to come Alex discovered a veritable hell. So did Barbara. So they continued, after all, to inhabit their own secret, sacred place; one in which the sensations they shared, of torment now and not of ecstasy, seemed as endless, as boundless, as time, every hour which passed, an eternity.

19

'Oh, Alex — could you just keep an eye on that for a moment to see that it doesn't *boil*, it has to *simmer* for ten more minutes and I must make this telephone call, I'm trying to get hold of Barbara.'

Yes, of course, absolutely. Get hold of Barbara. Oh, God, God in whom I don't believe, *have mercy on me*: you bastard, God, you complete and utter all-time sadist. I'm trapped here with the *sauce béchamel*, Claire is going to *get hold of Barbara*, my own, my goddess, and I'm going to have to overhear the whole thing. Impassively.

'Barbara? Oh, *brilliant* — I've been trying you all afternoon — how are you? Oh, good. Fine. Yes, they're fine too. Look, you must come and see us very soon — they've been asking for you! Yes, of course, I do understand.

'The reason I rang — specifically — you couldn't be interested in a little jobette, could you? Perfectly horrible, but cash on the nail. It's just — we have some friends who live in Chelsea with a five-year-old, a perfect little *monster*, their au pair has just walked out on them — I think they've managed to get through about three in the last year, *hopeless*: anyway, they're looking for someone who could collect the monster from school every day and take him home and give him his tea and generally keep him out of mischief until she gets home from work at about seven o'clock.

'And she'll pay five pounds an hour and fares. So I just thought *maybe* – anyway you could try it and see how it goes, what do you think? All right, her name's Louisa, Louisa Carrington – she's a darling, so is he, I can't think where little Fergus gets it from, I suppose he's simply been allowed to run rather wild. So here's the number – I should think she'll practically *go down on her knees* to you. She's *desperate*.'

I'll go down on my knees to you. I'll completely prostrate myself before you. I'll agree to be *buried in a deep pit* if only it will make a difference, if only I can have you. Desperate: you don't know what you're talking about, Claire – as usual; you know *nothing: this* is desperation, it has never truly existed before: it is born in me. It is borne by me. Although it can't be borne: *it is unbearable*.

'Well, as I said, you must come over – what? All right, super, yes, do that – I'll look forward to hearing from you. Don't leave it too long! Bye!'

'I hadn't realised that we had people coming—'

'Oh, Alex, you are *hopeless*. I reminded you this morning. Well, thank God you're back in time anyway. You've got half an hour till countdown. David and Sarah. I *told* you. I should have known you weren't listening.'

Alex went upstairs to see the children: Percy was still in the bath, playing with a battleship or two. He aired some of his opinions on matters social, educational and anatomical and then he said, 'I say, Dad,' – 'Yes,' said Alex, looking down at his tiny successor: 'I say, why don't we get Barbara to come and be our au pair, and then she could live here all the time: don't you think that's a good idea?'

'Barbara might not think so.'

'Oh, yes, she *would*. Will you ask her?'

'But Astrid's already here.'

'Yes, but Astrid is *homesick*. She told me so.'

'Well, that's very sad, but she has to get over it, because she wants to learn English: that's why she's here. Barbara already *knows* English.'

'She could learn something else instead. She could learn Latin.'

'Perhaps she knows that too.'

'No, she doesn't. I know because I asked her. I told her I was starting Latin in two years and could she speak Latin and she told me no. So there!'

'I shouldn't think she wants to learn it now, though.'

'She *might*. Will you ask her?'

'I say, Percy, old thing, it's time you got out. Have you actually washed yourself? With soap? All right then, pull the plug.'

Nothing so thin, so pale, so stick-like as a little boy. He seemed to be made of wire, his cranium full of tiny wheels and rods all turning, endlessly turning, producing their endless stream of speculations and conclusions, notes and queries. Quite soon they would begin to get their first serious tuning: *amo, amas, amat; amamus, amatis, amant*. The great mantra: around and around and around, until the end of time. God have mercy.

20

Fergus Carrington, that fiend in human form: what would she have done without him? He had silky ash-blond hair and a rosebud mouth and one saw quite a lot of his pink tongue because he so frequently poked it out at one. He also liked to kick and punch and pinch and to hit one with his satchel. He was a perfect little darling: exactly what she needed: what *would* she have done without him?

By the time she had him under something like control (it took only two months or so: she bribed him with the ten remaining marrons glacés, and when these were all gone, the National Army Museum) her yearning for Alex was only a dull constant ache.

The weather got colder; she took Fergus to Harrods and bought him the regulation navy blue overcoat and they had tea at Daquise on the way home. Fergus ate a large cream cake with a fork which he held in the correct manner, attracting comments full of extravagant admiration from two aged Polish women at a nearby table. Some of this admiration was directed at Barbara on the assumption that she was his mother and thus the person to whom credit was due, which was half true; she smiled at them briefly in graceful acknowledgement.

'They think you're my mother,' observed Fergus. 'It's a natural mistake,' said Barbara. 'What *are* you?' said Fergus. 'Tell me,' said Barbara. He thought for a moment and gave her a sudden suspicious sideways look. 'You're not an au pair, are you?' he said. 'I don't like au pairs.' 'No,' said Barbara. 'I'm not an au pair.' He thought again. 'I suppose you're just a friend,' he concluded. 'Yes,' said Barbara. 'Just a friend.' He sat brooding to himself for some time and then began kicking his heels against his chair and making a noise like an engine revving up, so his friend paid the bill and took him home.

It had been a creditable performance for a five-year-old boy, especially as it was he who, just as they were leaving, remembered the Harrods bag stashed away under the table. Just think if they'd forgotten that! 'What *would* I do without you, Fergus?' said Barbara. 'You'd be in really *bad* trouble,' said he.

21

Then the weather became seriously cold; Barbara and Fergus, coming home from school, ran all the way from the corner and up the steps and she unlocked the front door as fast as she could and they tumbled together into the hot, hot house and shrieked with relief as they took off their coats and their scarves and her gloves and his cap, which he threw into the corner, and was told to pick up, and Barbara hung it on the top branch of the coatstand.

And when Alex came home it was as dark as the shadow over his heart and as he went up the stairs to see his children Claire in the kitchen thought, vaguely, Alex is getting older; Alex is slowing down. Poor old Alex.

As it happened there was a poem (Anon., sixteenth century: another Tudor clergyman?) which having been quoted in one of the Sunday broadsheets was seen by both Barbara and Alex: perhaps even at the same moment:

> O western wind, when wilt thou blow
> That the small rain down can rain?
> Christ! that my love were in my arms
> And I in my bed again.

So that they both – perhaps even at the same moment – stared into the void of their loss and were half-consoled.

It was not long afterwards that Barbara heard, thanks to

her elder sister, of some people living near Bath who were going on a three-month cruise and wanted someone to house-sit for them, starting early in March. There then she was when the small rain down did rain: far from her lost love and the bed they had shared; not far, but a little farther, from the anguish (Christ!) of his loss.

Alex at about the same time had a drink with someone he knew at Macmillan, and over additional meetings on subsequent occasions managed to get himself commissioned to write a book on the black economy: all of his free time (except for the part which belonged to Percy and Marguerite) was thus taken up, and he fell asleep late every night too exhausted altogether to suffer the old torment of anguished, almost maddening, yearning.

PART III

22

The black economy book was now almost finished; there were just a few loose ends to see to before the final draft.

Alex, sitting on the daybed, was staring unseeing at the Caucasian rug. Funny to think that it was really because of Barbara that he had finally done what all journalists mean to do, and written a book. Men used to go out and explore the dark unmapped interior for less, he thought. And that – come to think of it – is what, after all, one could say I've been doing these last eighteen months: for the *terra incognita* of the world is all under our feet, these days; everywhere around us; it hides behind and beneath the allegedly known, the pattern behind the pattern: and there can be no end to it.

He got up from the daybed . . . *this bed is rather hard, isn't it; I do hope you haven't been sleeping badly . . . no, not at all: it's fine* . . . Christ! that my love were in my arms . . . and he looked out of the square window at the hawthorn tree.

Why did I come in here, he thought; what did I come in here *for*? And he looked vaguely at the bookshelves again, as if to find a clue. Then he suddenly remembered what it was: he'd come in here to look up a word in the *Shorter*, and he took out the A–M volume and opened it at the beginning, because the word he wanted was *abrogate*.

23

'Tom, I'm home! Where are you – oh! Ah. Sitting in the kitchen. And you've stolen a march on me, I see. Yes *please.*'

Serena sat down at the kitchen table opposite where Barbara had been. 'What's this?' she said, seeing Barbara's abandoned glass. 'Been drinking gin with the help, have we? Tut!' Tom looked so stupendously sheepish that she laughed aloud. 'Oh dear,' she said. 'Well –' said Tom. 'I mean, it seemed only polite . . .' 'To be sure,' said Serena. She took a swallow of the drink Tom had given her and got up. 'I say, let's go into the drawing-room, shall we?'

They sat down on the sofa; Serena kicked off her shoes and curled up next to Tom. 'Are the heavenlies around the place?' 'No – visiting Simon, so I understand.' 'Ah. Well then. Nice day?' 'Oh, yes. Usual thing. You?' 'A conference in Jessop's chambers.' 'Ah. The Meares thing, was it?' 'The same.' 'Go well?' 'Pretty foul.' 'Poor darling.' 'But you're the one who looks knackered. Everything okay?' She stroked the side of his head. He had that weary, bemused look, and he was gazing through the window at some far-distant and possibly even invisible point, whether in time or space who could tell?

'Oh, yes,' said Tom. 'Hmmm.' She went on looking at him and stroking his head, still holding her drink in her free hand – the one with the terrific solitaire diamond engagement ring on it. It was a cracker, that stone, and that natty Van Cleef setting. 'And how's our Barbara?' she said.

'Oh, you know,' said Tom. 'She's always the same. She's fine. She's – yes. She's – fine.' Serena laughed again. 'You don't fancy her, do you? Just a *tiny* bit?' Tom started. There was something about barristers: he'd noticed it often: they did tend to be disconcertingly, and sometimes even deplorably, direct. 'I say, Serena!' he protested. 'Steady *on*.' She laughed some more. 'I shouldn't be at all surprised,' she said gently. 'I'm not sure I don't rather fancy her myself.' Ye gods! Barristers! He shot her a look, so wonderfully compounded of dismay, disbelief, shock, and the suspicion that his leg was being pulled that Serena positively pealed. She put down her drink and put both arms around his neck. 'I really do *love* you, Tom,' she said. 'Isn't it funny? After all these years! I'd be so *very* sorry if you were to run off with Barbara.'

'Oh, she wouldn't have me,' said Tom. 'I'm quite safe; you really needn't worry. Anyway, you know I can't actually afford to. Not really.'

'No, that's true,' said Serena. 'So, look, do you think we might run to a long weekend away soon, once the babies have settled down at school? We might go to Paris, or Amsterdam, or that very flash hotel in the West Country that the Perelmans were telling us about, the one with the jacuzzis.'

'Gosh, yes, rath*er*,' said Tom. 'Perhaps there's a hotel in Paris with jacuzzis, what would you say to that?'

'Might that not be overdoing it?' said Serena. 'Oh, I think we can cope,' said Tom. 'All right, darling,' said Serena. 'I'm sure you know best. So we must really plan this properly. Do bring your work diary home tomorrow, will you? Now I wonder what that *delicious*

Barbara has left for us to eat tonight, I'm famished.' 'Er, I seem to recall there's a fool,' said Tom. 'I shouldn't be at all surprised,' said Serena, and she jumped up and went into the kitchen to see what else there was and put it all on the table and telephoned Simon's house to summon the twins. 'Ooh, smoked salmon,' she said, opening the refrigerator. '*Goody*.' And she ate some immediately, licking her fingers, her terrific diamond ring flashing in the light.

24

'Barbara? It's Andrew here — Andrew Flynn, we—' God help him, there was surely no need to remind her who exactly he *was*, after — had it really happened? Or had he not, after all, merely dreamed that he had sat with her on Primrose Hill and then moments later felt, tasted, smelled, devoured and devouring, that golden-skinned fairy — was it not much too good to be true? God help him.

'Yes. I know who you are.'

'Right.' A half second of that particular laugh, self-abnegating, self-exculpatory, nervous but not mirthless: a brief but complex sound which summed up an entire civilisation: not all those years' residence in a foreign land could banish it from the repertoire. Hurry up now and *say something*. 'Look, I just — how are you?' Oh, that skin, that voice; her hands: had he not merely dreamed the whole thing?

'Very well, thank you; and you?'

'Yes, I'm very well too. I was just wondering — I tried to get you earlier, as a matter of fact—' 'Oh, that was you, was it? I was upstairs, I heard the telephone but I couldn't—' 'No, of course not. No, it's nothing *desperately* urgent, but I just wondered if we might do something together perhaps tomorrow night, I'm afraid I have to be away at the weekend, but — you wouldn't feel like dinner or something, would you? If you're free?'

Oh, there it was: he hadn't really thought of it seriously before: she couldn't possibly be free, at twenty-four hours' notice, just like that, just for him. Not that voice, that skin, those hands; not for him. How dared he ask? And she was saying nothing − there was a silence, a silence even of embarrassment, that sense of the quest for the right phrase, the right tone, the right, polite, gentle, unmistakably definite dismissal.

Andrew: Andrew Flynn. Oh, don't you see? Can't you guess: don't you *know*? It's no good; it could not possibly be any good: can't you see? Does it have to be said? And yet, how? Oh dear.

'Well, I'm not quite − it's a bit difficult: I may be tied up until a bit late, tomorrow.' Another pause. 'There's a dinner party I have to do for someone.' Complete confusion. 'Oh.' Poor sod. He doesn't understand. Well, how could he. 'Look, why don't you − I mean, if you like − why don't you come round at eightish and then we'll see. Give me your number and I'll telephone you if I have to put you off. But it should be all right.' It's a bit of a mess but now that we've got this far I can see that the best thing to do is to sort it out a.s.a.p. 'I mean, if you like. Or we could leave it till next week. As you like.'

What's she trying to tell me? *What is she saying?* Only one way to find out. 'Yes, well, if you're sure − I mean, if you think −' because I can't now endure the idea of waiting until next week; I really must *know*: 'I'll come round at eightish then, and we'll see what you're in the mood for − will that be all right? Are you quite sure?'

'Yes, Andrew. I'm *quite* sure. As long as you don't mind − sorry I can't be more definite.' 'No, that's quite all right. Well, till tomorrow night, then.' 'Yes. Goodbye.' She hung up as soon as he'd had time to stutter his own valedictions, which might have been protracted.

She stared out through the French windows at the trellis and the tree-top beyond it, waving in the evening wind. I could go to the cinema, she thought; there might be something at the Everyman I want to see: where did I put that programme? It's probably in my bag, along with pretty well everything else. I'll go and look. But she didn't; she went on sitting, staring, staring, and thinking, until long after the film at the Everyman had started.

25

Claire and the children were coming back on Saturday, so if he, Alex Maclise, were really going to do the unthinkable, really going to go and see Barbara, there was only tonight, and it was getting too late to drop in on a woman you'd yearned after, lost for ever, seen by chance, been teased by – coldly, heartlessly – by whose memory you were now even more maddened than once you had been: now that she was so evidently no longer yours: might never have been: too late.

Or there was tomorrow night.

And that would be it.

And it was unthinkable; preposterous; it was a delusion of his maddened imagination that it was even theoretically feasible. As long as he could live through the next twenty-four-odd hours then he was safe; he would come out on the other side, the same dull stony place he'd inhabited before last Saturday night, safe: safe from his present madness.

The thing to do was to get on with one's work. The book still lacked a really satisfactory title: there: all a person *really* needs is an almost intractable problem to chew over. Alex began to chew.

There was a moment on Friday night, a crucial, wavering moment when Fate, her expression impassive, stood stonily in front of him waiting, daring him, implying (so one might have fancied) that either decision would be equally disastrous: a moment, crucial, wavering, almost sickening, when he might have left the club and gone straight to Belsize Park, have taken his chance, have exposed himself to whatever horror of rejection, ridicule, scorn might be implied in her behaviour at the party and afterwards: when he might have at any rate declared, with whatever result, his terribly reawakened passion. The moment – Fate watching, waiting, almost (but derisively) smiling – passed; he was safe. It was only much later, when the danger was entirely behind him, that he asked himself whether the ignominy which he had settled for was not, after all, the greater: but the question was now academic; one could therefore dare, now, to ask it.

The question did not, as it happened, remain academic. There was another message from Claire on the answerphone when he got home that night. It seemed there was some problem or other with the car; she and the children would not be returning, after all, until Sunday.

He had been given an apple, iridescently crimson without, which might or might not be poisoned; he sat, and began to contemplate it.

26

'These are for you.'

'Oh, Andrew.' Oh, Andrew, what *have* you done – no: what have *I* done? God forgive me.

It was a very big bunch of roses: it was actually three bunches all wrapped up together. They weren't (thank God for that at least) red, but they were an awfully dark shade of pink. Like lipstick. A faintly bluish, faintly decadent pink. They were beautiful. She just stood, looking at them, drinking them in. Well, they deserved it. Then she looked up at him. 'Come in,' she said, and they went inside.

She left him in the large room and vanished, returning with a vase and a half-full bottle of white wine which she put on the table. 'Do sit down,' she said. She vanished again and reappeared holding two glasses. 'Perhaps you could pour us a drink,' she said, 'while I put these in water.' She did it properly, removing the leaves at the base of each stem and splitting it.

Andrew sat quite silent, on a wicker armchair, watching her. She was sitting at the table; when she'd finished the flowers she moved the vase to one side so that her view of him was unobstructed, and then she slightly raised her glass to him and drank. 'How are you,' she said. 'It's been an age – what – two days, I think – since we last met: do tell me all your news.'

He laughed. 'Oh, I've nothing much to tell, I've had my head stuck inside a couple of learned journals most of the time – I've got rather a lot of work to do before the start of term.'

'Where are you, exactly?'

'King's.'

'Ah.'

'Handy for the river, you know, if it all gets too much.'

'That's true. Can't you swim?'

'Of course. But I've always understood that the water's so polluted that even if you don't drown you're bound to die of some kind of poisoning.'

'Now, that shows how long you've been away: didn't you know? It's been cleaned up!'

'Gosh, really?'

'No trout yet, but that may come.'

'Blow me down.'

'Why did you come back?'

He started slightly, unsure of her meaning; she saw his confusion. 'I mean,' she amended, 'to England? I mean, if you hadn't even known the Thames'd been cleaned up, then – the place has such a bad reputation these days, after all. I wondered why you'd come back.'

'Ah.' He ought to have understood. 'Yes. Well, there was this job. I'd always meant to come back if the right thing came up, and it did. So—'

'That was lucky.'

'Yes, it was. At least, I thought so. But then – well, then, when I'd got it, Janet – my wife – came along and told me she wouldn't be coming with me. So then I didn't feel quite so lucky. Especially when I realised that, of course, Mimi – that's my daughter – silly name, it's a nickname really – would be staying behind too. Sorry, I'm sounding awfully pathetic, aren't I. Shall we go out and have some dinner? And talk about something entirely different?'

'No, yes, all in good time. You see, you don't sound at all pathetic. It's just very very sad.'

'Yes, it has been. It was.' He paused for a moment, as if deliberating, and shifted slightly in the wicker chair. 'But actually – after I met you – it's the strangest thing, but suddenly it seems like something which happened long, long ago. I – I think – well, I—'

'Andrew.'

'Yes?'

'Andrew, I must tell you something. That is, I must say something.'

He looked at her doubtfully. 'Must you really?' He looked so sweet saying that; she almost wished she could say, no. 'Yes, truly. You see – about the other night—'

He was looking down at the floor: it was dreadful to be saying what she was now saying, but it had to be done.

'You see – I've been just a little loopy this past week.'

'Loopy?'

'Yes, loopy. Something happened, it's quite unimportant, but I haven't been quite myself. I'm not usually so – well, what's the word. Let's just say that what I did was an *acte gratuit.*'

'Yes, all right. But actually I don't believe there's any such thing.'

'Don't you?'

'No; it's a behavioural impossibility.'

'Yes, well, I think that's just my point, really. I mean, having performed one, I think I can agree with you, it's a behavioural impossibility. Which I can have no intention of repeating.'

'I see. Well – I – you wouldn't rather I went, would you?'

She had begun to realise, dimly, and now saw more clearly that he was a treasure.

'No, I wouldn't. I mean, if you can bear to be with me – if you can bear with me – please forgive me.'

'*Forgive* you?'

'You know what I mean.'

'All right: for the sake of the argument, I forgive you.'

'That aside – if you'd like to stay, and talk, or have some dinner, or both – there is some food here if you don't feel like going out, if you're hungry – I don't know what you feel like doing—'

'We'll go out, don't you think? I like being seen in a restaurant with a beautiful woman, it makes me feel rich and successful.'

He'd never seen her really smile before – not that smile, that very wide, enchanted smile, which made his description of her unexceptionably exact. She looked at him, the smile fading; there was a faint note of melancholy in her voice. 'You're awfully nice, Andrew,' she said. 'Really you are.' 'Yes, that's true,' he said. 'I'm glad you noticed. But I was sure you would, sooner or later – I knew you weren't completely stupid.'

'I'm just going to have a shower and change,' she said. 'I'm rather sticky, I only got back here just before you came. I won't be a moment. Then we can go. Have another drink if you like.' And she left the room.

27

When she came back, all dressed up and smelling nice, he was looking at a framed photograph on the wall. 'Who is this?' he said.

She went and stood beside him. Andrew had masses of self-control. 'That's my mother at the age of five,' she said, 'with her ayah.'

'Not really!' he exclaimed. '*Snap!*' She smiled at him. 'Not you too?' she said, wonderingly. 'Yes, me too,' he replied. They both laughed with astonishment. 'Were both your parents—' he said. 'Yes, both. What about yours?' 'Only my father's lot. My mother was merely Anglo-English. And still is, come to that.'

'So – of course *you* couldn't have been born there, could you?'

'No, not even I, old as I am!'

'But the memory lingers on,' she said. 'Or the melody, or whatever it is.' They were both looking rather grave now. 'Yes,' he said. 'How it does.' 'Shall we go?' she said. 'We might compare notes over a plate of – er – curry, or something.' He laughed. 'Something French, I thought,' he said. 'Someone told me about a place up in Hampstead – shall we see if we can get a table there? We might be lucky – it's fairly late now. I mean, you do like French food, do you? Or would you rather somewhere else? Do say.'

'Yes, I like French,' she said. 'Isn't it funny how we all like French?' 'No, it's not funny,' he said. 'It's only natural. After all, we're English.' She laughed. 'Come on,' he said. 'I'm ravenous.' He took her by the hand, but it felt perfectly natural, as if they were companions, and led her out to the car.

28

They were eating duckling and drinking white Burgundy, and somewhere a tape machine was playing a just-audible stream of the animadversions of George Shearing.

'Who are these people you work for?'

'Two lawyers, name of Hopetoun. And their two sons, aged thirteen. Twins, they are. Identical twins.'

'Are they nice, these Hopetouns?'

'Yes, very.'

'That's all right, then. What exactly do you do for them?'

'I get their dinner ready every night, from Monday to Thursday, inclusive. And I do a bit of cleaning – nothing much; not the heavy stuff. Someone else comes in to do that. And in return I get the flat, plus fuel.'

'No actual money, then?'

'I earn some outside: I do dinner parties at the weekends for people, and the odd lunch, and things like that. You see . . .' and so she gave him an account of her career to date.

Barbara's widowed mother had become ill with cancer some months before Barbara's finals, after sitting which she had gone home to look after her: her rather older sister, who was married to a Yorkshire GP, was fully occupied with their three children, plus assorted animals. After her mother's death, which had occurred some eighteen months later, Barbara had gone to stay with this sister for a month or two. 'I was feeling pretty useless, you see,' she told him. 'Quite helpless, actually. Couldn't get going on that career thing.' She paused, and then shrugged. 'Anyway,' she continued, 'we were into another recession by then. So I just felt I'd altogether missed the boat.' She paused again. 'I suppose I didn't even want to have caught it,' she added.

'Yes,' said Andrew. 'I see.'

'So then,' she sat up, smiling brightly, 'I saw this ad in the *Lady* for a mother's helper, in Kensington.'

'Ah, the *Lady*.'

'Yes, absolutely. And so I came to London.'

'And?'

'Oh, one thing led to another; you know. I just sort of faffed around – I just did odd jobs; and sometimes in between I signed on. And then, well – then fate brought me together with Fergus Carrington. Via Claire Maclise, as a matter of fact.'

'Ah.'

'You may well say so.'

She sat back and looked pensive. She had finished eating; she minutely adjusted the knife and fork on her plate. 'That was one of the things I taught Fergus,' she said, half to herself.

'Oh?'

'Table manners. I was very strict, you know.'

'That's good.'

'Yes. I mean, he knew what to do; it was just that I was the first person who'd had the time and the energy to insist absolutely on his doing it.'

'I suppose one has to do that.'

'I'm sorry – I'd forgotten – you—'

'It's quite all right. I'll have my chance next summer. And every summer.'

'So you will.'

Now they were both pensive, even sad. 'I was living in a room in Camden Town in those days,' said Barbara, trying to change the subject.

'Was that nice?'

'I wasn't awfully happy at the time. Fergus was a diversion, really; I don't know what I should have done without him. Anyway, then—' she broke off, inhibited by miserable recollection.

'Yes?'

'Then – well – my sister's in-laws had some friends living near Bath, who were going on a cruise, and wanted a house-sitter. So I went down there in the spring – when – yes, eighteen months ago, or so. And stayed in this glorious house. And when the people came back, I moved into a shared house in Bath and worked in a healthfood restaurant. And then when I got bored with that, I came here. I mean, to the job I've got now. Another *Lady* ad. That was almost a year ago. So now you know the whole. Sorry it's so uninteresting.'

'Not uninteresting,' said Andrew. 'Not in the least degree.' 'Well,' said Barbara, 'then lacking – lacking in structure, you could say. Not to say, purpose. Couldn't you?'

29

Andrew poured out more wine and sat back in his chair, looking at her. It was just such a tale as an angel, precipitated into the terrible world, might have related. He felt almost defeated by the pity of it all. 'Tell me about the future, then,' he said. 'What happens next?'

She thought for a moment and her face broke into an almost reckless smile. 'Well, there's always teacher-training,' she said. 'What do you think?'

Andrew was all but overwhelmed by her predicament; there seemed nothing useful he could say. 'I suppose it's been pretty hard on your generation,' he said. 'Going out into the world in the nasty 1980s.'

'Not wonderful, I suppose. Brilliant for some, of course.'

'And then, one mightn't want, after all, to be exactly the sort of person for whom it's been brilliant.'

'Still, you could argue that I've slightly overdone it.'

'Mitigating circumstances.'

'Actually, I do know someone who dropped out entirely on purpose. Conscientiously, so to speak. In fact he calls himself a conscientious objector, or did.'

'Who's that?'

'A chap in Bath. I met him because he was the gardener at the house I was minding. He lived by doing odd gardening work, and things like that, but once upon a time he'd been headed for the City.'

'Slight change of plan, then.'

'Actually, I think he did even put in some time in the City before ideology overcame avarice. He said one had to take a stand against *them*, and all that pertained thereto. He told me I was doing exactly the right thing, after all.'

'Ye-e-es,' said Andrew. 'Well, it can be problematical, trying to do the right thing. Knowing what the right thing is, for a start.'

'In this case,' said Barbara, 'I did the right thing – if I did – only by accident, as it were. So it hardly counts.'

'Perhaps that's the only way of really doing it.'

'Although one has to go on trying to do it, as occasion arises, doesn't one? Nevertheless?'

'I suppose one does. Nevertheless. Anyway – look – what about some pudding?'

30

Barbara, waiting for her coffee to cool, carefully unpleated the gold foil from a chocolate mint. 'Tell me exactly how your mother came to be born in India,' said Andrew at last.

'My grandfather was in the Indian Army. Both my grandfathers, actually. What about your people?'

'My father's father was ICS. And his father, and so on. My mother, however, was an unreconstructed English girl from the Home Counties; she actually met my father when she went out to India with the fishing fleet – in what was probably its very last incarnation, I dare say – just before the war. She had some relations out there. The way people so often did, one way or another.'

They exchanged an almost conspiratorial look. 'Anyway,' said Andrew cheerfully, 'it's jolly nice to meet someone who understands these matters, I must say.'

'A fellow initiate?'

'It's not a connection one dare mention before the laity.'

'God forbid.'

'Convinced as the laity is that the Raj was all exactly as portrayed by E. M. Forster in that wretched book.'

'To say nothing of the film of!'

'Good God, yes – there isn't a layman anywhere now who can't tell you precisely how it all was – fantastic, isn't it?'

'As a matter of fact,' said Barbara with a remorseful smile, 'it was once my modest ambition to be a historian of the Raj. I never really imagined doing anything else.'

'Why don't you do it, then?'

'Well, you know how it is – I rather lost my grip, not getting a good degree, and so on.'

'Mitigating circumstances?'

'That was my excuse. But now I'll never really know.'

'I shouldn't worry about that: just get on with it. Do an MA. Get to work!'

'Perhaps. Perhaps I will, next year.'

'I'll hold you to that.'

He would, too. 'I'll be your moral tutor,' he said. 'That's truly kind of you,' she replied; and in this moment, remembering their anterior meeting, they both half-sadly, half-ruefully smiled. He took her hand for a moment. He was ready at this moment for the long haul; for whatever time and effort might be necessary. He frowned very slightly. 'It's funny being back,' he said. 'In England.'

'It's a fairly funny place, I suppose.'

'All things considered, quite possibly the very funniest there is.'

'Yes, I wouldn't be surprised. When you consider.'

'Have you ever been to India?'

'No – but actually – do you remember the conscientious objector? His name is Gideon, by the way. Gideon Ainsworth. Well, Gideon had this plan – he was due to come into a trust fund of some kind this year—'

'Oh, is he now?'

'Just a very tiny one. Or so he said. Anyway, he always said that as soon as he did, he was going to organise an overland trip to India. You know, that thing. People are doing it again now, you see.'

'Oh, are they? That's good.'

'Yes. So, he used to say that I should come too, and a few other people he knows. He'd thought about it all quite thoroughly.'

'Was he planning to pay for you all, then?'

'Oh, no. But actually I've got a few things I could sell – furniture and things. My sister's got them in her attic.'

Andrew thought for a moment. 'Yes,' he said. He was quite emphatic. 'You really should go if you possibly can. Sell up and go.'

'Have you been?'

'Yes, I've been. No, but you really should, you know.' This was moral tutoring, as he lived and breathed.

Barbara smiled at him, swept along by his certainty, which she did not yet share. 'Will I find God?' she said.

And although she'd never before seriously imagined that she really could go off to India like this, she suddenly understood, now, that she quite possibly would: that it really was a thing one could do: and the awful, insupportable grief which had lain in her heart like a stone for the past several days (a grief reborn, redoubled) seemed to lie by just one degree less heavily. Andrew smiled at her. 'Well, we'll see,' she said lightly. 'Gideon's probably forgotten by now, anyway. Or he might have changed his mind altogether. We'll see.' And now she even hoped that Gideon Ainsworth had not changed his mind, and had remembered: for what else, after all, could she reasonably do, now, but go far, far away?

'Gideon isn't, after all, essential,' said Andrew. 'You could find another companion. Or even go by yourself.'

'Yes,' she agreed. Even this seemed possible. 'I could, at that.'

'There you go, then,' said Andrew; and they sat smiling at each other, like two people in a state of perfect agreement.

31

At first there was only a long silence while they stared at each other, standing quite still on either side of the threshold, weak with shock and a sort of dread – he, truly, as unprepared as she for the awful actuality of being in the other's presence – mute and helpless; terrified.

Alex at last spoke. 'Well—' he said; he looked down at the ground, at the stone flagging with which the area was paved; he looked up again at Barbara's expressionless face. 'Can I come in?' Still silent, she stood aside to let him enter and pushed the door to behind him. 'This way,' she murmured and he followed her down the corridor and into the large room. They stood in its midst, looking at each other, helpless, terrified.

'Why have you come here?' she said.

She had folded her arms; she stood there, staring at him, waiting. He could not explain himself to this maenad. He looked around the room: 'Do you mind if I sit down?' he said; she shrugged slightly and he sat down in the wicker armchair. He was almost trembling. He crossed his legs and then gestured slightly toward the other chair, as if inviting her to occupy it, and after a slight hesitation she did so, but with a sort of impatience, as if she were saying, What the hell. Her arms were still folded.

He felt suddenly exhausted, almost as if he might cry. Nothing that he was feeling, had felt, in the past few minutes, in the time since he had rung her doorbell, had been foreseen, or foreseeable.

It had all begun quite differently, it had begun with that morning's awakening out of and into a wonderful clarity: a conviction that he would (he should, he must) of course go and see her this evening: that there was no question left to ponder: that he would quite certainly, as a matter even of propriety, simply drive over to Belsize Park, get there around five o'clock, if she were not there find a pub to wait around in, and go on trying her doorbell, every hour on the hour, until it was too late to hope that she would return that night.

So there had only remained the day to be lived through – the long, long day, whose final hours had suddenly strangely rushed past him at an almost-too-dizzy speed: and then he'd arrived here; of course he remembered clearly which white stucco-fronted house it was, the flight of steps to the front door, the urns with the geraniums either side, the number: 51. The barred front window of the basement flat, the yellow-painted door next to it. Five o'clock. He'd found her first time. No pub, no waiting: just this unforeseen, unforeseeable terror.

He looked across at her: the chair she sat on was drawn up almost to the table; on this, on her left, stood a vase full of roses – dozens of them, lipstick-pink, half-opened, some even beginning to hang their heads. An even-less-foreseeable unease was added to his terror. Roses . . . dozens of them . . . and he had brought her nothing, nothing but himself, with his terror, his dread, the extremity of his desire to be with her. He'd spent half the day wandering around Camden Passage, trying to find the one thing, the one magical jewel or gewgaw which would have been right, which would have been at once rare and splendid enough and yet free of all hint of presumption: it didn't, it couldn't, exist. Every other idea had been futile, even flowers, in the circumstances, had seemed futile.

'I'm still waiting,' she said.

'Waiting?'

'You haven't answered my question,' she said. 'Why have you come here?' She had unfolded her arms; she sat, still looking at him, one hand against the side of the vase full of pink roses. He looked at her, full as he was still of terror, dread, unease and a creeping hopelessness.

'I wanted to see you,' he said.

32

She made an effort; it was very difficult. 'You wanted to see me,' she said, as if reflecting. She was examining the roses, touching one, holding up its hanging head. 'I don't understand,' she said. 'Suddenly, out of the blue, you wanted to see me. I don't understand.' He took a packet of cigarettes out of his breast pocket and shook one out and offered it to her. She shook her head. 'Do you mind –?' he said. She shook her head again. There was an ashtray on the table; she pushed it towards him and he got up and fetched it and returned to his chair. 'It isn't actually sudden,' he said. 'It isn't out of the blue.' He inhaled and blew out some smoke.

She remembered that tweed jacket, that brand of cigarettes. Everything was the same, except that they were here, now, alone together and absolutely estranged. She felt suddenly exhausted, and could almost have cried: she, too. She felt as if they had both lost their souls and were condemned here together.

'At the party,' she said. How to go on: to speak about that terrible night. 'You didn't want to see me at the party. Or afterwards. Why now?'

He stared at her. 'At the party,' he repeated. 'At the party *you* didn't want to see *me*.'

'How can you know that?' she cried. She had sat up straight; her face was flushed. 'How can you say such a thing? What could you *possibly* know about what I wanted or didn't want at the party or anywhere else? You hardly spoke to me! And then you hardly listened to what I said.' She broke off, overwhelmed with the horror of what she was recollecting – the sick excitement of seeing him, suddenly, across the room; the casual tardiness of his eventual approach to her, the irony in his voice, his manner: the implicit declaration of utter indifference: the pain, the unendurable pain. The appalling, half-hysterical effort to conceal it throughout the evening, the awful heartbroken effort, the grinding, abominable *pain*.

It was he who was appalled, now. What was she saying, what extraordinary scene was this which she was showing him: what horror, what hope was now perversely revealed to him? He could barely follow all the implications.

'I – but surely—' and he broke off, trying to see, to recollect, exactly what had happened: what each of them had done, had said: 'I didn't believe it could really be you,' he said; 'it never occurred to me, it never *could* have occurred to me, that you'd be there. I didn't even know you *knew* the Carringtons.'

'I used to look after Fergus,' she said. 'You might have known that. It was via Claire that I got the job, after all.'

He was silent, half-remembering.

'In fact,' she went on, 'I probably wouldn't have been there, wouldn't have been asked – I don't actually see them these days, not since they moved to Battersea, except that I ran into Robert and Louisa at the NFT, a few weeks beforehand.'

'But then . . . you must have realised that I might be there. Or Claire, or both of us.'

'In fact, I was fairly sure you wouldn't be. That was why *I* was. Louisa asked me, when we were chatting, had I seen Claire lately – we were just making conversation, the way one does, and I said, only on the telly, and she said, unfortunately she wouldn't be at the party, because she'd be on holiday then in Brittany. I naturally assumed that meant all of you.'

'Claire and I don't take holidays together any more,' said Alex. 'Too much of a bad thing. Well, okay, not *bad*, but not *good*. I take the children skiing in the winter, she takes them to a *plage* in the summer.'

'I see.'

'When I first saw you, at the party,' said Alex – oh, that moment, that astounding, that delirious, moment, as it were of hallucination: Barbara in a grey-green dress, with something silver on it – were there silver threads in it? – talking to someone, someone else, noticing him, going on, talking, talking to someone else, someone who leaned over her, and said something to make her laugh: Barbara, indifferent to him, unreachable.

'Yes?'

'I got the impression you weren't awfully eager to speak to me,' said Alex.

'What did you want me to do?'

'You seemed perfectly happy to go on with what you were doing,' said Alex.

'You are *stupid*, Alex,' said Barbara. 'I never noticed before.'

'No,' he said, very evenly. 'We never knew each other at all well, did we? Other than in the Biblical sense, of course.'

'I think you've just shown me how extremely stupid you actually are,' said Barbara. 'And crass, and contemptible, and what a complete waste of time this meeting is, and I think it's probably time we brought it to an end. You said you wanted to see me: I hope you've seen your fill, because if you haven't, *tough*.' And she got up. She had folded her arms again, and she walked past him towards the door.

33

Alex got up. He did not follow her, but stood still, looking after her. At the door she turned, and looked at him. 'Well?' she said. 'If you're quite ready, I'll just see you out.'

Alex made a terrible effort: he had not known that such an effort could ever be either possible or necessary; it was new to him, it was beyond all imagining; he had been projected into another state of being and thinking and it had to be dealt with or he might be damned for ever. 'Please don't,' he said. His expression was stricken. 'Please let me finish.'

'What else can you possibly have to say?'

'Forgive me.'

'For what, exactly.'

'What I just said—' he looked down at the floor, ashamed, appalled; he looked up again; he looked at her, into her eyes. He was speechless; he saw the enormity of what he had said. They gazed at each other. She came back across the room and stood in front of him. She touched his stricken face. 'Alex,' she said; she was looking at him very gravely. 'What has happened to you?'

'Nothing,' he said. 'Absolutely nothing. Until last Saturday night. Since then – you see, I thought – even if I'd known I should be seeing you, I might have thought, well, why not, where's the problem? I'd stopped thinking of you – one just turns to stone, after a while. One has to go on, somehow.'

'Is that the way to do it?' asked Barbara sadly.

'I don't know. But it's one way. It was the only way I could find.'

'Of course you had more to see to than I,' said Barbara. 'Yes,' said Alex, 'I had.' There was a silence; Alex had taken her hand, he was holding it very firmly. He looked down at her; his face now looked almost stern. 'Have we established, then,' he said, 'that we were each mistaken, at the party, in believing that the other didn't want much to speak to one, as it were?' He was looking seriously, searchingly, into her eyes.

'Then there was afterwards,' she said.

'Yes, well – you'll have to give me some credit for trying,' he said. There was still that stricken expression in his eyes. 'I did at least take you home.'

'But not alone,' she said. He saw what she was saying. 'That couldn't be helped,' he said. 'Andrew hadn't a car; he'd come there with me. I couldn't simply leave him to it.'

'No,' she said. 'I suppose not. But I didn't know that at the time.'

'Is that why you were so sarky in the car, then?' said Alex. 'I was furious,' said Barbara. 'I thought you'd done it deliberately.'

'You mean, avoided being alone with you?'

'Yes.'

'God help us.'

'And then—'

'Yes?'

'Since then, there's been the whole week,' said Barbara. 'It's been as long a week as I've ever had.'

34

'So – let me make quite sure I've got this straight,' said Alex. 'And do you think we might sit down again?' He led her by the hand which he was still holding over to the divan bed and they sat down on it. He offered her another cigarette and although she almost never smoked, this time she accepted. He fetched the ashtray and returned to her side. 'You were sure I didn't any longer care about you,' he continued, 'and that I didn't want to be alone with you, albeit sufficiently the gentleman to see you safely home from Battersea on a Sunday morning: is this accurate so far?'

'Yes.'

'And yet you thought I might none the less come here to see you the next day, or soon thereafter.'

'I hoped you might. For the first few days, I *hoped*.'

'So in fact, you suspected that my indifference was merely apparent.'

'I hoped it was. During the first few days, I *hoped* it was.'

'And you hoped also, of course, that I would entertain the same suspicion about *your* feelings.'

'I thought my feelings were fairly plain.'

'You amaze me.'

'I sang all those love songs.'

Alex almost roared. 'You know, I believe that's the first

time you've ever made me laugh,' he said; and he began again. Barbara began to look woebegone. 'It's not *that* funny,' she said. 'Yes it is,' he said. 'And furthermore, I was quite sure you were doing it just to wind me up.'

'Well, I was, of course, *as well*,' she said. This time he was almost helpless. Somehow in the last minute or so they had both sprawled back across the bed. Alex half sat up. 'So,' he said, 'you wanted to see me – leaving aside *why* for the moment: is that altogether admitted?'

'Do get on with it,' said Barbara, 'whatever it is you're up to.'

'All right then,' said Alex. 'Tell me why.'

'I wanted to know how you were.'

'You might have found out at the party.'

'No. It had to be in private.'

'All right. You've found out how I am. Now what?'

'I haven't. You've told me nothing. I want to know *much* more.'

'Why?'

'I'm simply inquisitive.'

'Who gave you those roses?'

'A friend.'

'Some friend.'

'Yes.'

'Of course, you must have friends.'

'Haven't you?'

'They don't give me roses.'

She got up and went to the table and broke off (she had, in fact, to bite through the stem, because it was very tough) a rose leaving a few inches of stalk; she came back and carefully put it into his buttonhole. 'There,' she said. 'They do.' He took her hand again. 'Why didn't you come before,' she said. 'What took you so long?'

'I was afraid,' he said. 'I was quite sure you didn't want to see me: I've told you.' 'Why did you come, then?' 'I had to see you anyway. No matter what.'

35

It was much later; darkness was falling.

'Tell me the story of your life.'

She told him, in a few sentences – there seemed so little time. (Two years ago, there had been none.) She sketched an outline of the army brat childhood, the lonely reserved adolescence, the awkward and, finally, over-shadowed university years; and the rest. 'I can't think why you want to know all this,' she said.

'How long have you been living here?'

'About a year.'

'Where were you before that?'

He was remembering, vividly, the room in Camden Town. His arms tightened around her. 'Oh, Bath—' she began; but he started to kiss her again, and then there was no more talking for some time: but afterwards, he remembered her last words. 'Tell me about Bath, then,' he said, lighting a cigarette.

'I was minding a house for some people who went on a cruise for three months.'

'Rich people, eh? Nice house?'

'Divine. Lovely garden. And they had a Bösendorfer.'

'What's that? Some kind of dog?'

She shrieked, and then she enlightened him. 'The gardener used to play it, too,' she said. 'He was a pretty mean pianist, actually. We used to sing those

Gershwin songs, and other stuff.'

'Some gardener.'

'He was a conscientious objector.'

She told him about Gideon Ainsworth. 'I suppose he fancied you,' said Alex gloomily.

'No, men of my age never fancy me. Only older ones.' 'Yes,' said Alex complacently. 'Those young blokes are too green. You'd be wasted on them.' Barbara turned her head and looked at him. 'Were you green?' she said. 'Yes,' said Alex. 'Green as grass. My salad days, when I was green in judgement, cold in blood.' They were silent. 'What are we going to do?' said Alex. '*What in God's name are we going to do?*'

36

'Nothing.'

'What?'

'*Nothing*. What *can* we do?'

'You know perfectly well what we can do.' He sat up: then he suddenly noticed the roses again. 'By the way,' he said, 'who exactly gave you that lot?'

Barbara, still lying down, looking up at him, considered what to say. 'As a matter of fact,' she said, 'Andrew Flynn gave them to me.'

'He *what*?' Alex, appalled, stubbed out the cigarette. 'Andrew *what*?'

Barbara said nothing for a second, and then she took his hand. 'Andrew wasn't to know,' she said. 'He wasn't to know that anyone – that you of all people – might have a prior claim.' Alex was silent. 'And neither, come to that, was I,' she added.

'So?'

'He took me out to dinner last night.'

'I must say he's a damned fast worker.'

'Well—'

'Come to think of it he always was. These quiet scholarly types are the ones to watch.'

'He's probably rather lonely. He's just had a divorce, for God's sake.'

'So he has. That's no reason – well – well, why not –

why not, after all. Oh, God. What *the fuck* are we going to do?'

Barbara sat up. 'I suppose we could wait,' she said. 'Until the coast is clear. If you like.'

'What do you mean?'

'Didn't you tell me that you were obliged to stay with Claire until Percy's settled in at secondary school? Well, how old is he now – eight? So it's only another five years or so.'

'I wouldn't begin to expect you to wait for that long; it's preposterous.'

'Could *I* expect *you* to wait that long? Or at all?'

'Oh, me – I'd wait for twice as long: what else have I got to do? Whereas you—'

'Yes, I – well: we'll just have to see what happens, won't we? We'll have to trust what happens to God, I suppose.'

'God.'

'This being one of those cases where there's absolutely no one else *to* trust.'

What could one say to that? Even Alex could say nothing to that. But Barbara was remembering the conversation of the night before: 'Will I find God?' she had asked, in all levity. 'I might find God,' she said, almost to herself. 'That's not how it works,' said Alex. 'You don't find God: God finds you.'

'Either way.'

'Meanwhile, I note no mention's been made of the alternative to waiting until Percy's got himself sorted out.'

'What's that?'

'You know what I'm talking about.'

Barbara frowned. 'Let's not go through that again,' she said. Alex lit another cigarette. 'There has, in fact, been a very material alteration in the situation since our last discussion,' he said.

'Oh?'

'As regards Claire.'

'What?'

'I have good reason to believe that Claire now has a lover.'

'Oh, yes?'

'So what about us?'

'It makes no difference whatsoever to *us*.'

'You can't possibly be serious.'

'I am. You must see that.'

'I wish I didn't.'

'I'm sorry, Alex.'

'Are you really?'

'Yes. I really, I truly am. I do see that my being your secret lover might in the circumstances be perfectly all right for someone else. It just wouldn't be for me. For us. Whatever Claire's situation. I can't have a secret liaison with you – I *can't*. I'm so sorry.' She turned his face towards hers and looked at him. 'I'm so very sorry,' she said. There were tears in her eyes. They looked at each other for a long time. 'So am I,' said Alex. 'It's a complete and utter bitch.'

'You might find someone else. You could, easily.'

'Yes, I know.'

'Well, then—'

'Well, we'll see. We'll wait and see.'

'Yes. We'll wait, and we'll see.'

'Let me know if you stop waiting, won't you?'

'You too.'

'I can't believe that two people, two human beings, are having this conversation. It's a bad dream.'

'Life is a bad dream.'

'Come now.'

'It is, it truly is. Oh, there are some good bits, but on the whole it's a bad dream, where things just happen completely beyond one's control. We're all basically *helpless*.' Barbara was sitting up, staring into the face of naked Reason. 'All there is in the end,' she said, 'is – is – simply – trying to keep one's hands clean – and it's difficult. It's probably impossible. But—'

'You're wrong. All there is, is whatever real connection one can manage to have with another soul, another lost soul – that's the only thing one can hope for. And you're turning your back on it, actually rejecting it, for the sake of a mere scruple.'

'It isn't *mere*. And we couldn't have a *real connection*, as you put it, as long as this scruple exists.'

'We're fucked then, aren't we?'

'Not thoroughly, Not finally. God may deliver us.'

'Him again.'

'There's no one else who can help us here.'

Alex laughed. 'So God gets the last word,' he said. 'Even when you don't believe in him. Or especially then. What a sportsman – I do believe the bastard's an Englishman after all. One of the old school, that is. Must be the last one left alive.'

'As long as he *is* alive.'

'Let's hope so,' said Alex. 'As long as he's our only hope.' He was laughing no longer; he wasn't even smiling. 'Sod it,' he said. 'Sod everything: especially God.'

'Don't say that.'

'All right. I take it back, just for you.' Suddenly he was weary: 'Listen,' he said, 'what would you say to some dinner?'

They tidied themselves and went out to eat at a restaurant in Belsize Village. The hour was late; the place was almost empty. 'We're always the last customers,' said Alex. 'Have you noticed?' They laughed together, restored by food and wine, and held hands, and Alex believed he would, in fact, wait, preposterous as it might seem; and Barbara did too.

'I might just be going away quite soon,' she told him. 'I might go to India.'

'Never.'

'I might.'

'Please don't.'

'What difference would it make?'

'Something might happen to you.'

'I'll be fine.'

Alex said nothing for some time. 'I'll give you my numbers,' he said. 'In case you ever need me, or anything. Anything at all.'

'Thank you.'

'Don't thank me; I'm doing it for me.'

'Okay.'

'How could I reach you?'

'You couldn't.'

'In case I need to tell you that I've stopped waiting.'

'Oh, yes – of course. I'll give you my sister's address; you could always write to me care of that.'

Not that either of them envisaged ever sending such a message: it was only that each was bound to believe it to be possible that the other might wish to. 'Well,' said Alex, putting the slip of paper which Barbara had given him into his pocket, 'I suppose I ought to say in the circumstances that I don't look forward to hearing from you.' Barbara gave him a weak smile. 'Likewise,' she said. He took her hand. Having no discernible future, they had not another word to say.

37

Claire was looking through her diary; Alex handed her her drink and sat down with his own. The show was on the road again.

'Are you off to Scunthorpe this year?'

Claire looked up, surprised. 'Fancy your remembering Scunthorpe.' She very slightly stared at him, her eyebrows raised.

'Can't think why. Must have seen something about it in one of the Sundays.'

'Hmmm. The machine's been turned on good and early, then. Yes, well, since you ask, I may well be – it isn't firm just yet. That's one of the things I have to sort out this week. I should call Lizzie first thing – oh, and that reminds me! You didn't mention that Barbara turned up at that party of Louisa's. You really might have told me. That girl's a godsend: if I do go to Scunthorpe – if she's free, and I hope to God she is, she'll solve all my problems.'

'How do you mean?' Blankly.

'She might come and mind the kids again, obviously. It was an absolute nightmare finding someone to do it last year; if I hadn't been able to borrow Lizzie's au pair I would have been sunk.'

'Perhaps she's busy.'

'Of course, I don't suppose you thought of asking her

what she's up to these days, much less got her telephone number. Did you even talk to her?'

'Oh, I had a word or two.'

'A word or two. Honestly. You men. She's a *godsend*. Well, I'll try to get the number from Louisa: although she couldn't seem to find it when we spoke before.'

'I told Andrew you'd ask him round for a meal some time. Show him the kids.'

'Oh, did you now. Well, I suppose I'd better, then. I expect you do have his number, have you? Well, that's a start. Poor old Andrew, eh? A bachelor again. Now, I wonder who we might know – oh! of course! Barbara! It's perfect. I'll ask them together. Marvellous. Now who else should I have to make up the numbers – who do we owe?'

Alex was dumb, horrorstruck; then relief overwhelmed him. Of course Barbara would politely decline any such invitation. He was safe. They were safe. Their secret love was safe. Their secret love glowed within his heart; it illuminated the night. He finished his drink, and stared at his wife as, her blonde head bent, she continued to look at her diary, making occasional notes. His salad days. Shakespeare. But this, alas, had been no vegetable love. Marvell. With my body I thee worship. Thomas Cranmer. So one supposed. 'The English Renaissance,' he said. 'That was *the* time for Eng. Lit. Do they ever discuss that up in Scunthorpe?'

'Of course not. What an idea.'

'Just wondered.'

'What do you know about the English Renaissance?'

'Oh, nothing. Nothing, nothing, nothing, nothing, nothing.'

'Honestly, Alex. How's the book?'

'Oh, the book's fine. Shooting it into Macmillan's in a week or two.'

'Oh, good.'

'Yes.'

'Well,' said Claire, closing the diary, 'I think that's my lot for the day. Time for bed. Good night, Alex.' 'Er, good night.' And she was gone. Alex sat, staring into the past, and into the future, for the present, he thought, did not bear examination.

PART IV

38

'Truly, Louisa, I could throttle him. The *jackanapes*.'

Louisa was laughing so much she had to sit down on a bench. Her brother Alfred Ainsworth (younger by a few years than she) stood moodily nearby, slashing at the occasional fallen leaf with his tightly-rolled black umbrella. He turned to her. 'When you've finished,' he said. This only made her start again. 'Oh, Alf,' she said. 'Where would we be without you?' She was still giggling. Jackanapes, forsooth!

'That's just my question. Where, indeed?'

'God knows. But as it is—'

'You depend on me far too much. On my probity, my sobriety, my solvency and, not least, my tireless and I might even say miraculous patience.'

'I? Now when did *I*—'

'All right, perhaps not you personally. Not, anyway, in any material sense, at least not recently. But morally speaking, I sometimes have the feeling that you're just as dependent as Gideon, damn his juvenile, irresponsible, knavish impudence.'

'Now I like that! You are addressing, may I remind you, the wife of an official of the Bank of England. You are talking to the mother of a child – and no ordinary child at that, as I think you will agree.'

Louisa realised too late that this tease would be quite

lost on Alfred: for Alfred's opinion of his nephew Fergus was not altogether commendatory. The child had charm, and even intelligence, but his character seemed formed on the lines of his Uncle Gideon's, which could in Alfred's view be matter only for deprecation, if nothing much stronger. Thus the conference at present in session: he having summoned Louisa to the Embankment Gardens on this autumn evening for the purpose of discussing Gideon's present situation – this venue being reasonably close both to Alfred's own place of employment (he was at the bar) and Louisa's (in a famous shop in Regent Street). They had met here for the same reason more than once over the past decade, when they had taken on years and family responsibilities, while Gideon, youngest of the three, had continued to nettle and astound, disconcert and appal his elders. The death of their father several years ago had left to Alfred the task of expressing – if not indeed of feeling – vexation and contempt (those pre-eminently paternal sensations) in addition. His umbrella stabbed at another leaf. 'Come along, Louisa,' he muttered. 'That's enough sitting about. Let's get on.' Louisa rose, and continued to trip along the path beside her brother. She took his arm.

'The thing is, Alf, that I don't *really* see why you're in such a stew: Gideon's done nothing *wrong*.'

'Wrong? You don't think it's wrong, to squander that trust fund – or at any rate a large part thereof – on some damnfool trip to India – India! – at *his* age – what do you imagine the purpose of its being locked away until his thirtieth birthday was, if not to avert just such a folly? He was meant to have *grown up* by the time he came into it. It was intended to go towards the school fees, for God's sake.'

'Ah, yes, the school fees.'

'Well – yes – it's all very well for you to talk like that, in that blasé *je m'en fiche de vos school fees* manner, I must say! Do you still mean to send Fergus to Eton? Supposing they'll actually have him, that is.'

'Come now, *mon frère*. Gideon, *voyez-vous*, has no children, after all. He isn't even married, for goodness sake.'

'Exactly.'

'You wish he were, do you?'

She had him there. 'I wish he were in a position even to consider it,' said Alfred, with what seemed like genuine regret. Louisa looked at him. 'Wouldn't it be an awful bore,' she said, 'if we were all like us two? A family needs one non-conformist, doesn't it?'

'He doesn't half overdo it.'

'Come now.'

'Look at the score. Sacked from school for smoking pot—'

'Don't call it pot, darling. Only hopelessly square people would call it that.'

'*Pot*. Next: left Oxford without taking his degree – a wicked waste of time, that, to say nothing of taxpayers' money. Then what – oh, yes. We pull every string in the book to shoehorn him into that berth at Lloyd's: and the rest I think you recall. Royal College of Music, or was it the Royal Academy – it makes no odds – Morocco, Greece – then this flight into Somerset, or whatever the county's called these days – look, I know that the country's been going to the dogs, I grant you that, these past umpteen years or so—'

'More torn apart by jackals, don't you mean?'

'– but that's no excuse for becoming an absolute wastrel. Why doesn't he try to do something constructive?'

'Well, he has been. Do be fair, Alf. All that gardening! If that isn't constructive—'

'Gardening, hah! And now this. Squandering his patrimony. Well, just let him try to come prodigal son-ing back to me, in a year or so. He may be surprised at the reception he gets.'

'You'll put a ring on his finger.'

'*What?*'

'Have you forgotten? That was one of the things the father did, when the prodigal returned.'

'Oh, did he. Well, you won't catch me putting a ring on Gideon's finger, I'll tell you that.'

'Actually I think he probably will settle down after this India business,' said Louisa, looking reflectively ahead. Alfred sighed. 'One can but hope so,' he said wearily. 'And that's another thing. Who are these people he's going with?'

'Oh, some chums from Bath, and so on. I think he mentioned a girl called Barbara. I really know nothing about them. They'll be five altogether, I understand. Safety in numbers!'

'We had really better know who they are, and where they come from.'

'Send them each a form to fill in,' said Louisa mischievously. 'In triplicate, of course.'

'Very funny. It is as I said: morally, you are just as feckless as Gideon. Surely – as the wife and mother you are, as you earlier reminded me – you can see that we ought to know with whom Gideon is crossing half the planet.'

'Well, so we shall in the fullness of time,' said Louisa comfortably. 'He's coming up to London at the weekend to stay for a few days or so, or even until he leaves – I'm not quite sure what his plans are. Anyway, I'll have plenty of time to interrogate him then.'

'Well, you might have said so sooner, and saved my grey hairs.'

'In fact, as soon as I do know what his plans are, I'll arrange a lunch, or a dinner, or something, and you can interrogate him yourself.'

'Yes, that would be best.'

Louisa could see that Alfred was quite serious. Well, so be it, she thought. Feckless, was she? Feckless. It sounded something like carefree. Oh, how she wished she were.

39

The intercom buzzer sounded; Andrew picked up the receiver.

'I say, Andrew? Alex here. Shall I come up? Are you busy?'

'No, not at all; ascend!' He released the lock, the street door slammed shut and Alex was almost immediately at his front door. Andrew ushered him into the still-new, still-bare sitting-room.

'I was in the neighbourhood and had some time to kill, so I thought I'd call in.'

'Ah; flattered, I'm sure. Kill away.'

'Do you want to try this grass? It's meant to be Colombian.'

'Let's see, then.'

Alex made a spliff and lit it. 'How are things?' he said. 'Keeping busy?'

'You bet.'

'Been anywhere? Done anything?'

'Here and there. Round and about. Took a girl to the cinema the other night.'

'Anyone I know?'

'Actually, yes. Barbara, actually.'

'I see. Nice work.'

There was a silence. Andrew in an instant saw, and Alex saw that he saw, but neither showed this seeing by even the slightest flicker of an eyelid. The silence for a moment continued, and then Andrew spoke.

'Claire telephoned – I suppose you know. I'm bidden to dine on Thursday.'

'Oh, yes, I had been told. Yes.'

'She said she'd been in touch with Barbara; that she'd thought of asking her along too – she knew we'd met at the party, of course. But Barbara'll be up in Yorkshire at that juncture.'

'Oh, will she.'

'She's selling her set of chairs in the style of Thomas Chippendale, et cetera. They've been in her sister's attic up there.'

'Short of cash, is she?'

'She's realising some assets, so as to go to India.'

'Ah.'

'Leaving pretty soon, as a matter of fact.'

'Should be fun.'

'The really funny part is, the chap who's organised the whole thing – he's bought an Espace, a bunch of them is doing the overland trip – this chap, one Gideon Ainsworth, turns out to be Louisa Carrington's younger brother.'

'You don't say so.'

'Yes. Fact. Pure coincidence; Barbara got to know him when she was living in Bath, last year. Never made the connection, of course, never having known Louisa's maiden name – and even then – anyway, all was revealed after he came up to London the other day, and gave her his London number, which she called all unaware, only to find young Fergus answering the telephone – awfully disconcerting.'

'Absolutely.'

'Small world, eh?'

'Come to think of it – we know Louisa's other brother:

you mightn't remember him, if you ever met him – Alfred: wasn't at the party; I suppose he and Lizzie were still on holiday. Yes. This Gideon must be the wanton younger brother of whom one's heard now and then. And so – he's going off to India, with Barbara—'

'And some other people. Five of them all told.'

'I see. Five Go Overland to India.'

So Barbara's gardening friend was Alfred and Louisa's brother. The shock – the dismay – of learning that she was indeed going away – and soon – was wonderfully mitigated by this fact: he would have a link to her: he knew someone with whom she was almost intimately connected. It was nothing much, but it was infinitely better than nothing at all. She was going away, but she was not going right away – not absolutely and altogether beyond his knowledge. It seemed almost miraculous. But – oh God – would she not let him have a word, just one word, of farewell?

Andrew was laughing. 'As a matter of fact,' he said, 'this party of five consists of three chaps and two chapesses: no dog, you see. What a joke. Hope they've all read the books.'

Alex dimly perceived that Andrew, too, might be feeling pain, might be concealing the pain of loss: of an additional pain, an additional loss, at that. What a life it was, indeed: what a world. He was still feeling almost stunned. 'Crazy,' he said. 'It's a crazy world, *mon capitaine*.'

Andrew had stopped laughing. He flicked some ash off the end of the spliff. 'Yep,' he said decisively. 'It is that. Crazy, but crazy. I say – good word, that. Onomatopoeic.'

'I don't think that's quite the term you want.'

'You know what I mean.'

'Yes. Yes. *Crazy*.'

★

She did give him a few words, to fill the miles, and the months, even the years – even the eternity: who knew? – which separated them. He received the telephone call late one afternoon, on his private line at the office.

'Please don't say anything, Alex – I just wanted to tell you – I'm going to India. Quite soon, actually. I just wanted to say – well – you know.' She sounded quite calm and quite rational. So did he. 'Yes,' he said. 'Me too.' 'I'll tell you if ever I stop.' Still calm; still rational. So was he. 'All right.'

'And – please tell me if ever *you* stop.'

'All right. I'll tell you if I ever stop.'

'I must go now, Alex. Goodbye.'

'Yes – my—'

She rang off before he could find another word to say: she was gone again – perhaps for good – just like that. Alex sat, stunned, dazed with longing and loss and dreadful misery: until some demon in his heart raised its head and made him look – for just a moment – objectively at himself. How can this thing be happening to me, he thought: to me! Perhaps I've lost my mind: perhaps I'm mad.

He sat on, accustoming himself to this new state, this madness which he both felt and, by observing it, repudiated. From then on, for a very long time, Alex mad and Alex sane continued to live together. Sometimes the one stared the other down, but they managed to co-exist well enough. There was no serious conflict. But he began to see life in its entirety as an irredeemably irrational construct, and he wondered how this knowledge was to be endured for all the time that remained to him. Then he gritted his teeth, and went on playing the game, and nobody could have imagined what was in his heart.

40

The video diary began to appear on the television screens of the nation within ten days of Gideon's – and his companions' – departure.

Not a word had Gideon said to anyone (other than said companions) of this project – 'Alf is absolutely *gobsmacked*,' Lizzie told Louisa, having seized the first opportunity to telephone her sister-in-law, on the day following the screening of the first episode. It was aired – in the first instance – immediately before *Newsnight*: one could hardly have missed it. 'Serve him bloody right!' said Louisa. 'I always told him Gideon would come good, but of course he refused to listen to *me*.'

'He'll probably get a book out of it, too,' said Lizzie. 'Emma's been on the phone to me already, wanting to know if he's agented.'

The trip unwound its by turns weary, weird and hilarious length, from the Hook of Holland to Delhi, over several successive weeks, in the course of each one of which an enthralled nation was able to watch an edited version. The sales of camper vans rocketed, and young and less-young workers the length of the country prayed for redundancy – so long as adequate compensation was in that event due. Others, already free to do so, sold everything they possessed at the nearest car-boot sale, signed off, and left (in or on a variety of vehicles, depending) immediately. It was not as if no one had ever done this journey before – far from it; it was just that, as someone observed, this particular version put the overland-to-India journey *on the map*. Twelve-year-old Janey Beaufort of Hammersmith opened a savings account – having first compared the interest rates of all those on offer – into which she henceforth deposited all but a tiny fraction of the money she earned each Saturday morning doing household chores for her mother, strictly with a view to following in Gideon and party's footsteps (so to speak) at her earliest opportunity, and a similar scheme was formed in the mind of eight-year-old Guy Dawlish of Clapham, who fretted at some length over the relative merits of National Savings Certificates vs. the more accessible Investment Account.

It should not be supposed that either of these children, or any others, viewed the diary in its pre-*Newsnight* slot: it was repeated (by popular demand: Auntie always listens) on Sundays, just before the joint comes out of the oven. Tapeheads everywhere pored over it at their leisure, and a bootleg edition was soon in circulation.

'You must admit,' said Louisa in due course to Alfred, 'that our Gideon shows remarkable qualities of leadership, and organising and management abilities of no common order. I'll bet ICI and BP and that lot can't wait to get their hands on him.'

'Humph,' said Alfred.

'To say nothing of his diplomatic skills. The FCO will probably want him to run courses for them.'

'Sure to,' said Alfred, in a tone of desperate irony.

'And by the way,' continued Louisa relentlessly, 'you never told me he could speak Arabic!'

'As far as I'm concerned,' said Alfred, 'he can't.'

'Well, it seems to get the job done,' said Louisa. 'Uncle Gideon,' put in Fergus, 'is one *real* cool dude.' And the whole nation – or that very large part of it which watched the video diary, in one time slot or another where not both – would heartily have agreed to that. It was not often that Fergus spoke for everyone, but he was entirely aware of having done so now, and savoured the moment. *Everyone*, that is, excepting his Uncle Alfred. Fergus was entirely aware of this, too. He turned to the silent dissenter. 'Don't you think?' said he. 'In a pig's ear,' said Alfred.

41

It was all over. In the very last episode, the party having reached Delhi, ownership of the Espace was transferred to four Indians, recent graduates who – now headed for post-graduate courses in the UK – were to make the same journey in reverse. They, too, had a video diary contract, and all the essential equipment. 'We, however, have – alas – no ladies in our party,' their leader told Gideon. 'But you know how it is, here.' He sighed, and smiled. 'Too bally idiotic for words, but there you are. We grin and bear it. I say, do you know Mark Tully, by the way?' 'Only terribly slightly,' said Gideon.

The chapess who was not Barbara now flitted immediately away to Goa, where she may still be; one of the chaps who was not Gideon soon went, thereafter, to check out an ashram he'd heard about, and having done this much, checked rather extensively in. The remaining chap, one Charles Wesley, undiverted by either of these particular extremes, remained of the party, which now made the first of many railway reservations, and began the truly serious business of travelling over the great and most marvellous land of India, and was not much heard of for many moons thereafter.

42

'Heard anything from young Gideon lately?' said Alex to Louisa one evening early in the spring.

'Not really lately. But you know what the Indian posts are like.'

I wish I did. Oh, God, if you knew how I wish I did.

'The last letter I had – it was just a scrawl, really, on an aerogramme – must have been about six weeks ago,' Louisa went on. 'Everything seems to be going well. Fallen utterly in love with the place, and so on.'

'Is he going about on his own now, then?'

'Oh, no. Still with the others. Barbara, that is, and Charles. I suppose it's a lot more amusing that way.'

'As long as they get on.'

'I imagine they must do. Anyway, I don't expect they'll stay too much longer, what with the hot weather arriving.'

'They could go up to the far north, of course. Darjeeling, Simla, that sort of thing.'

'Yes,' said Louisa vaguely, 'that's true. Well, bully for them. I mean, it's quite marvellous, don't you think? I wish I'd done it. But I will, too, one of these days.'

'Yes,' said Alex, 'yes, I dare say you will.'

'Dear Barbara, though,' said Louisa, 'I'm so glad she's still with Gideon. A really *excellent* girl, don't you think? Even Alf had to admit Gideon'd shown good judgement there.'

'Yes,' said Alex, 'yes, I suppose he did.'

'Perhaps he's fallen in love with her by now,' said Louisa brightly. 'I do hope so.'

'Or perhaps the other chap has.'

'Charles? No, I'd really much rather Gideon did. And Gideon is better looking.'

'Perhaps they both have.'

'Yes, that's more than likely. How could they not? She's certainly rather lovely, in that old-fashioned sort of way. I thought she looked quite wonderful on the telly.'

'Yes, I suppose she did.'

'Well, then.'

'Well – yes – well, we'll see.' Wait, and see. Oh, God, spare me this.

'Yes, indeed! Let's hope some more post gets through soon.'

'Absolutely.'

Oh, God. Oh God oh God oh God. And even this is not the worst possible suffering. Alex consoled himself with this reflection; he became almost cheerful. This, now, is not the very worst. She is still – for all I know – waiting. And so am I. Mad, but hopeful. By the grace of God.

43

Alex and Andrew had taken to playing squash together, regularly every Tuesday night. 'We must be mad,' said Alex, flopping on to a bench and wiping the sweat off his face. 'Whose bloody ridiculous idea was this?'

'Yours, as a matter of fact.'

'Ah. Well, then, it can't be as bloody ridiculous as it seemed, after all. Come on, back to work.'

They played on until their time ran out, and then repaired to the nearest pub. 'This is what it's all about,' said Alex, drinking cold beer. Andrew drank silently. 'Yes,' said he after a while. 'It all basically comes down to this.' 'My round,' said Alex, and he got up and went to the bar.

After he had returned and begun on his second pint, Andrew reached into a pocket and pulled out a preternaturally flimsy-looking sheet of paper. 'Got a letter from young Barbara in the week,' he said. He was staring steadily ahead, the hand holding the letter resting uncertainly on the table in front of him.

'Oh, yes.'

'Yes.'

'Everything all right?'

'Seems to be. Like to read it?'

'Oh – no – none of my business, after all. As long as she's all right. And the rest of them. Gideon, and whatsisname.'

'Charles.'

'Whoever. Still together, then?'

'Not for much longer. Hot weather. Party's pretty well over. Barbara's going on to Australia.'

'Oh, really?'

'Yes. She met some people from Sydney who've asked her to stay as long as she likes – you know what these Australians are like.'

'Open-hearted. Open-handed. Generous and hospitable.'

'To a fault.'

'Can one be?'

'I suppose not. In any event, they've apparently got a large house, in a place called – let me see—' he looked at the letter – 'Balmain. She's given me the address. She'll be getting there round about now, actually. Then she means to find work of some sort. Waitressing, or whatever turns up.'

'Jolly enterprising.'

'Playing it by ear.'

'She'll – yes. She – what about the others? They going to Australia too?'

'Oh, no. Charles is going to America. Gideon's coming back here, to write his book.'

'Ah.'

'While he's still hot.'

'Yes, I see.'

'Of course,' said Andrew – and Alex, once again, glimpsed for a moment his friend's predicament – 'Barbara will probably come back too, fairly soon. I mean, I imagine she'll start to miss the old place sooner or later.'

'You only stayed away for ten years, after all.'

'That was different.'

'Yes. Well—'

'Mimi comes here quite soon. Summer hols. My turn to parent.'

'Ah.'

'Strange old world, isn't it?'

'Crazy.'

'Yeah. Have another?'

'No thanks, mate. I'm due at the *chez* about now.'

'Right you are. Shall we?'

They got up and left the pub, and Andrew gave Alex a ride home: it was not far, but at even five times its length the journey might have been as silent, preoccupied as each was with his own thoughts. He's a good sort, old Andrew, thought Alex as he walked up to his front door and let himself into the house. He's all right, is the old Alex, thought Andrew, as he drove away. Poor bastard.

44

Mimi arrived at Heathrow in the care of a BA stewardess, with three juvenile-sized pieces of matching luggage, the smallest of which she was able to carry herself, and wearing a Radcliffe sweatshirt. Andrew fought back tears, and swept her up in his arms. 'It's good to cry,' said Mimi.

After five days in London he took her to a rented cottage in Herefordshire, near his parents and — less near — his sister; catering became less of a problem. There was a walk every morning, without fail. 'That's an elm,' he told her. 'Now rare. And that chap's a beech.' And so it went on.

On Sunday morning he took her to church: she made a fist of singing the hymns. Not that he'd have dreamed of such an outing, left to himself. But he wanted the child to receive an indelible impression of everything — anything — one could call English — so long as there should still remain anything one could call indelibly English. (The liturgy had been vandalised, of course, but they hadn't done anything so barbarous to the building itself, and they were still using Hymns Ancient and Modern.) 'How do you do, Vicar. Yes, just visiting — down from London. Yes, yes indeed, thank you.' And on to the next punter. 'Dad? I'm *real* hungry.' 'Well, isn't it a good thing we've got a roast dinner waiting for us at Grandma's?' 'What's a roast dinner?' 'You're about to find out!'

And Yorkshire pudding, and gravy. As only the English can, or would. And raspberries, afterwards, that his father had grown, and that Mimi had helped to pick. Well, he did his absolute best; so did they all.

'So, Mimi, what do you think of England?'

'England's *cool*!'

But at night she got homesick, and cried for her mother. Andrew cuddled her, and brought her hot milk – which she didn't like, until sugar was added to it – and read her a story, until she at last fell asleep. Then he went and sat in the low-ceilinged cottage parlour, and looked out into the darkening country night, and thought: crazy. Will it – can it – ever come right – really right – now?

45

Zoë and the Bazza didn't seem to mind how long Barbara stayed – 'Feel free!' they said. She found a waitressing job in a restaurant ten minutes' walk away: she earned the most stupendous tips. She started saving money, so as to go around Australia on a bus, and she gave Zoë a suitable sum each Friday to cover rent and board. 'Well, if it makes you feel better,' said Zoë.

There were lots of people coming in and out, even staying for a few days or so, in this household. It was that sort of as-yet-childless ménage. 'Hey there, Barbie,' they said. 'How are you doin'?' Offers of sight-seeing drives, of weekends in houses in the Blue Mountains and up the north coast and down the south coast came in a steady flow: people couldn't have been kinder. And the food was superb, and the weather, of course; and the scenery. 'So how are you liking Sydney?' the affable new acquaintances asked her. 'Oh, it's Paradise,' she assured them.

And what should I do in Elysium, she asked herself: my lover, he is in Illyria. Well, at any rate, Albion. She was wrenched by homesickness; and by the further qualification, that Alex, after all, was not, precisely speaking, her lover, and at last, having sufficiently considered all this under the relentless antipodean light, she was devastated by the realisation that it was, after all, beyond all likelihood that Alex and she would ever now be lovers again: that the notion of his waiting so long for her, if not also she for him, was entirely exorbitant, and could no longer, truly, be entertained. Blinking in the unforgiving glare, she stumbled through the awful sunlit days.

She ought in any event to write to Andrew – she'd even bought an aerogramme for the purpose. She'd bought it some weeks ago. Here was a pen. She sat at the table in her bedroom, contemplating once again the impossible task, defeated by an encompassing sense of the futility of her existence, looking out through the window at the fabulous ultramarine of the Harbour where the white-sailed boats merrily tacked in the prevailing wind. What should she do in Elysium, or anywhere? Overwhelmed all at once by a despair which was entirely new to her, Barbara began suddenly, silently and uncontrollably, to weep. She was discovered thus by Zoë who, having knocked perfunctorily on her door had entered the room immediately; concealment was impossible.

'Oh, God, Barbie – is it something I've done?'

'No – oh, no – no of course not – it's *nothing*—'

'Or Baz? He's a tactless blighter, the Bazza. Just tell me.'

'No, no, really – you couldn't be kinder, either of you – I'm so lucky to—'

'Oh, God, poor old Barbie.'

Zoë crouched awkwardly by Barbara's chair, an arm around the girl's shoulders. 'I know,' she said. 'It's probably just culture shock, that's all. It's a killer, isn't it?' Barbara said nothing; she was still crying too much to speak more than a few words at a time. Zoë continued to crouch beside her, looking upwards, her large dark eyes full of apprehension. At last Barbara's tears abated and she sat, looking down at her hands, while she folded a fresh Kleenex tissue into ever-tinier squares. 'It's nothing,' she said. 'Really.' 'Nothing?' 'No, really. It's just – I suppose it's just, that I don't really know what *to do*.' 'To do?' Barbara shrugged helplessly. 'I don't know what I'm doing,' she said miserably. 'With my life.'

'Oh – no one knows that! Join the gang!'

'No, but – I mean – I just – I don't actually *belong* anywhere. All I do is drift along – I've never even had a proper job—'

'And you're complaining?'

Barbara managed a very pale smile. 'I can't go on in this way,' she said. 'But I – really – I don't know what else to *do*.'

'This is so sudden,' said Zoë. 'I mean, I thought you were so free – you and Gideon and Charles – the nineties dropouts – great – I thought—'

'Oh, that was then. Now—'

'I suppose you're missing Gideon, eh? I mean, he's quite a guy.' She gave Barbara a questioning sideways glance. 'Oh,' said Barbara, shrugging, 'yes, well, a bit, I suppose. I mean, Gideon – I mean, we're not—' and she began to cry again: two large tears ran down her cheeks and then she began to weep in earnest. She'd never meant to tell, and never previously had told, anyone, anywhere, about Alex: but now, since it was the only possible release from an unendurable sorrow, she related, very briefly, her tale.

46

'Oh dear oh dear,' said Zoë. 'Oh, God. Well, there'll always be an England.'

'How do you mean?'

'Well, for God's sake. I mean – no, look, forget I said that. But it all sounds so mid-Victorian. Poor Barbie. I mean, this guy, this Alex, for a start. What's all this staying-together-for-the-sake-of-the-kids stuff about, when we're at home? Are you sure he isn't just fobbing you off?'

'Of course not!'

'Well, all right, sorry – oh, God, what have I said?'

Barbara had started to cry again. 'You don't understand,' she sobbed. 'Alex isn't like that, he—' Alex is entirely truthful and entirely honourable. How did she know this? It was true none the less. *It was true.* 'All right, I believe you; please don't cry.' Zoë gave her another tissue. 'Here,' she said. 'That's better. See,' she went on, as gently as she could, 'even if he believes he's got to stay put, I mean, fair dinkum, even then – he could be wrong, you know. I mean, if him and his wife have gone so cold on each other – well, what sort of an example of adult relationships is that for two impressionable kids? For another – what is it – five years? Four? Whatever. Ye gods. So. This Alex. I don't suppose it's occurred to him that the kids might actually be better off with him and his wife living apart, has it? It has been known, you know. God, we know dozens of divorced parents – kids thriving – no one bothers about that stuff these days: there are worse things to worry about, believe me.'

'Yes, yes, I know. But it's just — it wasn't for me to urge that point, you see.'

'Oh, wasn't it?'

'No, truly it wasn't.'

Zoë was silent, half-exasperated, half-dumbfounded; Barbara sat, staring in miserable reminiscence at her hands as they folded another tissue into ever-tinier squares. 'Well,' said Zoë at last, 'that seems to leave only one alternative then, which is for you two to be lovers. Go for it, Barbie-doll. You've earned it.'

Barbara almost smiled. 'Yes,' she said.

'What's the problem then?'

'I can't.'

'You can't?'

'I can't. *We* can't. Oh, I suppose Alex would be happy enough — for a while, at any rate. But even then — you see—' and Barbara made a huge effort, looking up, looking into Zoë's eyes, straining as never before to articulate the entire truth: 'you see,' she said, 'it just wouldn't *do*. It wouldn't be good enough, it would be unworthy. The deception, the secrecy, the untruth of it — it wouldn't be what we *are*, it wouldn't be *good*.'

'Oh, God.'

'I'm sorry.'

'You English.'

'Oh, no — it's not we English — it's just me. Most of the English would agree with you, I dare say. I don't know.'

'All the same. Oh, God. Look — do you love this guy, or don't you?'

Barbara looked at Zoë again. 'Love,' she repeated. 'Well — obviously — but you see: what I think is, that you have to find out what it *means*, as time goes on – I mean, you start with one thing, but it keeps changing. And that's just it, you see: we wouldn't find out – it might even stop being love altogether – if we had this secret relationship; if we were deceiving other people by having the relationship at all – it wouldn't, actually, be real. It wouldn't be the real thing. It wouldn't really be *love*.'

'This is probably too metaphysical for me.'

Barbara looked downwards in misery. 'It's just the way I am,' she said. 'Yes, I can see it probably looks stupid. It probably is stupid.'

Tears started to roll down her cheeks again. Zoë, feeling a genuine and even profound pity, put her arms around the girl. 'Perhaps it'll work itself out, somehow,' she said. 'You've just gotta keep the faith, babe.' 'Yes,' said Barbara, crying silently. 'Yes, perhaps it will.' She wiped her eyes. She had spoken bravely, without hope – for it was time to release her confidante. 'Anyway,' she said, 'I must look for something to do. That's the immediate problem – I see that now. I mean, it's been wonderful – India and everything – I've been so lucky, truly – Gideon, and Charles, and you and Bazza – but – I have to *do* something.'

'Well, you will.'

'It's just a matter of deciding what.'

'No problem.'

Barbara could almost have believed her. She managed a glimmering smile. 'No,' she bravely, but hopelessly, agreed. 'None. Oh, God.' Zoë patted her shoulder encouragingly, while Barbara wiped away the last traces of her tears. She looked up again at Zoë. 'Isn't it strange,' she said, 'the way we always say that? *Oh, God*: you'd think we actually meant it.'

'Don't we?'

Barbara looked at her, startled. Zoë, a believer? 'Only joking,' said Zoë.

'Oh,' said Barbara. 'Yes, of course. Silly me.'

'Yeah. Silly you. Say, what about a cuppa? A nice cuppa, and a nice spliff.'

'Wouldn't say no to that.'

'Yer on then!'

Barbara followed Zoë downstairs, through the endless-seeming darkness, bravely and without hope; *Oh, God*, she said to herself, *God help me*. And that was when she saw it. She was almost winded with the shock – it was like being suddenly knocked over, right off one's feet. She began to laugh: she was laughing so much that she had to sit down, helpless, and lean her head on the kitchen table. 'Good God,' said Zoë, 'what is it now?'

Barbara laughed even harder, then at last she looked up. 'I've just seen it,' she cried. 'God! He *does* exist!' 'She,' said Zoë. 'Whatever,' said Barbara. 'It's that person, that thing, that's there when you say *Oh, God*. There'd have to be something there, actually *there*, or you couldn't say it, could you? You *couldn't*.'

'I reckon not.'

Zoë began to laugh too, and that's how the Bazza found them when he came in: laughing their heads off. 'What's going on here?' he said.

'Barbara's just found God.'

'No, God found me.'

'Same thing.'

'Is it?'

'Has to be.'

Bazza started laughing too: they all, all three of them, had a jolly good laugh. It was absolutely the funniest thing that had happened for an age. God!

47

Lizzie Ainsworth (who was a television producer) had run into Simon Beaufort (who was a television director) down at the Beeb, and on learning that his wife and children had all gone off to the Périgord without him (he having been detained in London by work, contrary to the original plan) had asked him round for a meal; this done, she had invited Alex to join them – 'Poor old Alex,' she explained to Alfred. 'I mean, there he is, rattling around in that enormous house, summer after summer, while Claire and the kids lark about on a French beach – might as well give the poor old darling a square meal while it's going.'

'Poor old Alex,' said Alfred, 'is probably glad to be rid of Claire for a bit. Probably perfectly happy, actually, even if he misses the kids, which I wouldn't assume.'

'All the same,' said Lizzie. 'Poor old Alex. Poor old Claire, come to that – poor old things, both of them. Rotten luck.' 'They might as well get divorced, really,' said Alfred, uncorking a bottle of white wine.

'They can't, they're staying together for the children; at any rate until Percy's at Winchester.'

'Westminster.'

'Whatever: still a long way off.'

'What a horlicks, eh?' Alfred poured out some wine and tasted it. 'Poor Claire,' sighed Lizzie, with genuine feeling. 'Poor fiddlesticks,' said Alfred. 'She's probably having it off with some novelist on her free afternoons. It's Alex I'm sorry for.' 'Alex could be in the same boat, of course,' said Lizzie. Hardly were the words out of her mouth when the doorbell rang. 'Whoops,' she said. 'That'll probably be him now.'

Alex's appearance, having precluded further speculation about his love life, might also seem to obviate it: Alex certainly had nothing of the aspect of the lover. He had – as generally – that look, both weary and feral, of the man who has no partner. Still attractive, too, thought Lizzie. Doesn't even need much cleaning up. Poor darling. She kissed his weary, feral cheek. He smelt all right too. He handed her a bottle of Margaux. 'You poppet,' said Lizzie; Alex gave her a brief smile which might have melted a stonier heart. 'Well now,' said Lizzie, almost disconcerted; 'what will you have to drink?'

Simon Beaufort arrived twenty minutes later with a bottle of Graves which they opened to drink with the meal, which was almost ready; at last they sat down.

First they talked about Alex's black economy book, due to be published in the autumn. 'Giving it all they've got, are they?' asked Simon. 'It's getting a launch party,' said Alex.

'Oh, where?'

'White's.'

'What a joke. Who's coming?'

'All of you, I hope.'

'Naturally. Anyone else?'

'The Chancellor may put his head around the door for a moment or two.'

'Never!'

'So the rumour goes. His PPS is not unhopeful.'

'What a riot, I can't wait. I must have a new dress.'

'Must you?'

'Alf, darling, don't be a killjoy. I'll pay for it myself.'

'I'm afraid you'll have to.'

Alex thought it time to divert the conversation from his own concerns and turned to Simon. 'What exactly are you up to these days?' he said. Simon told him, and the talk became rather shoppy. 'I tell you what, though,' said Simon, suddenly remembering, 'I saw that Gideon fellow the other day – your brother, isn't he, Alf?'

'Alas, yes.'

'Just listen to him! Poor Alf. "Alas" indeed. Where did you see him, Simon?'

'In a restaurant. Which one could it have been, now? One of those places.'

'*Ah, les restaurants de Londres.*'

'I remember who he was with, though, he was with that Emma Whatsit – you know – that agent, the one they call The Fox. And a BBC producer I vaguely recognised.'

'Well, I must say that takes the biscuit – as far as we're concerned the villain is meant to be holed up virtually incommunicado in the cottage in Dorset writing his absurd book.'

'Don't be silly, Alf, he's almost finished that. He'd just buzzed up to town for the day, obviously. In fact, I think I know why.'

'Well, I wish you'd tell me. Not that I care, one way or another. But it is my cottage.'

'Or, as it were, ours. Yes, this is a most material point. He has no right, having borrowed it—'

'Exactly: borrowed, you notice. Not rented.'

'—having borrowed it, to leave it for a whole day without telling us.'

'Well, you know what I mean. Here he is, in London after all, not a word to us—'

Lizzie threw up her hands. 'I don't know what to do,' she said despairingly to Alex and Simon. 'Ever since his wastrel younger brother whom he never tired of excoriating became a decent respectable media star Alfred has been in a perfect tizzy. His exasperation has, if anything, actually increased. Behold, the relentless logic of the legal mind.'

'Well, it's all so utterly spurious,' said Alfred. 'Not to say, completely *unreal*. All this fame and success. It's not as if he's had to *work* for it.'

At this, they all (except Alfred) howled with laughter. 'How true!' they cried. 'How terribly true!'

'Anyway,' said Lizzie, recovering herself, 'I'll tell you why he was in that restaurant with The Fox and that producer – I think I know which one it was, too – it's because he's probably going to be doing a new series for the Beeb.'

'Now I've heard everything!'

'No kidding.'

'Some sort of travel thing?'

'Got it in one.'

'Do we actually want another travel thing?'

'Look at those we already have and I think the answer may come up before you in bright shining lights.'

'That's what Gideon is after. His name in bright shining lights.'

'Don't take any notice of Alf. Yes, it sounds quite good: sort of video diaryish, but more structured – obviously – a sort of independent travellers' guide, but all shot on the hoof, so to speak.'

'Could be classy.'

'Just one major little problem.'

'What's that?'

'They need a girl. Or, you know, a woman.'

'Plenty of those. Should be able to find one.'

'Yes, but Gideon's rather keen to have one in particular.'

'Oh, is he? Well, a TV contract beats a box of Milk Tray any day.'

'Depends on the woman, I would have thought.'

'That's my Alfred. You'd swear he was serious, wouldn't you?'

'I am.'

'No, but tell us, Lizzie – who's the particular girl Gideon wants?'

Thus Simon. Alex sat dumbly, holding the stem of his glass, unable even to eat, looking down at the tablecloth. It had a pattern of thick blue and thin red stripes on a white ground. He thought he would never forget it. He knew – he had been seized by a chilling prescience, a mutation of the cold horror which had entered him as soon as Gideon's name had first been mentioned – what was to come.

'Yes, he wants that girl Barbara, the one he went to India with,' said Lizzie. 'You remember – did you see the video diary?'

'Oh, of course. Barbara. Now which was she – the sylph, or the rather more voluptuous type?'

'The latter.'

'Hmmm. Could she do it?'

'Something of a moot point, as she's presently in Australia.'

'Does Gideon want this show or doesn't he?'

'I understand that as soon as he's got their agreement in principle he'll put the hard word on her to get herself

173

back here pronto and strut her stuff.'

'Perhaps she'd rather have the Milk Tray, after all.'

'Not if she knows what's good for her.'

'Can't see how Gideon could be good for anyone, with or without a box of Milk Tray up front,' said Alfred. 'Ah, well,' said Lizzie. 'Nell thinks he's *fabulous*,' said Simon. His younger daughter Nell was nine years old. 'She's got a picture of him on her wardrobe door – I see it every time I go in to kiss her good night; no wonder I recognised him in that restaurant.'

'The thing is,' said Lizzie, 'speaking as a pro, I do think that Barbara girl could have something as a presenter. Huge novelty, for a start. She's so authentic. And she's certainly attractive enough – rather gorgeous, really, in her way. They can do something about the clothes and so on. It's just a question of whether she can do the business.'

'Well, someone had better remind Gideon about the story of Citizen Kane and that singer creature.'

'Or the other way around.'

'No, no, I tell you – it isn't like that. At least I don't think so. No, Gideon genuinely *a* thinks she can do it and *b* equally to the point believes they *work*. As a team. The chemistry is right.'

'Ah, chemistry.'

'No, not *that* chemistry. Ye gods, you men—'

Well, Simon, actually. Alfred and Alex had both remained more or less silent: Alex wholly so. In fact, he must speak soon or his silence might begin to seem significant. 'I should think he knows best,' he said. 'After all, he's spent a lot of time with her, going to India, and then all around it. Must know her pretty well.'

Brave, brave Alex; and no one there to know it: no one, anywhere. 'Just so,' said Lizzie. 'That has to be right,' said

Simon. 'And she him,' said Alfred, drily. 'I dare say she'll turn him down, in the event.'

'Oh, I don't know so much,' said Lizzie. 'She hasn't got a lot else to do, from all one can gather. Anyway, we'll see.' At this moment naughty Henrietta, who was meant to be asleep, came into the room in her crumpled nightdress, blinking in the light and asking for water – that ancient ruse – and by the time she was dealt with the topic had changed altogether. Alex was out of danger. *In extremis*, but out of all danger.

All danger; all delight; all hope – yes; yes: that (now he saw it clearly) was the place he'd come to, again – now, when the knowledge was, just, endurable. Barbara would not, and could not, wait for him – even if he could (as of course he could) wait for her. He might hope no longer, if he had not stopped hoping already. He had returned – could anything be more cruel, more absurd? – to the dull stony place he'd inhabited before that Carrington party – or its aftermath – of a year ago. Welcome, summer, with your green leaves, your deserts. He was conscious of a silence and looked up. Alfred was offering more wine. Yes, he might as well get soaked; he wasn't driving. 'They want me to do another book,' he announced. 'About the Lloyd's thing.'

'Oh, well done. Have you said yes?'

'Not exactly.'

'You really might as well, why not.'

'Yes, you're probably right. Why not? Got to keep busy.'

Oh, God, thought Lizzie, poor old Alex. It just isn't fair. She said as much to Alfred after their guests had departed. 'When you think,' she said, 'that Louisa and Robert actually met each other at Claire and Alex's wedding – which they wouldn't have done, otherwise. And look how happy they are. Whereas Claire and Alex, the cause of their happiness – as it were – are not happy themselves. It really is so unfair.'

'Well, now you know all about life,' said Alfred. 'It's unfair. And talking of that, how do you come to know so much about Gideon's present circumstances, of which you haven't mentioned one word to me? I knew nothing about this new television programme.'

'Oh, I hear things on the street,' said Lizzie. 'And anyway, I spoke to him on the phone the other day.'

'You never told me.'

'I didn't want to annoy you unnecessarily.'

'Huh.' Alfred sighed. 'Gideon,' he muttered to himself. 'When I *think*.'

'The thing is,' said Lizzie, 'I do think it would be nice if you could be a *bit* pleased for Gideon. Or *about* him. Or both.'

Alfred considered this proposition. 'Well,' he said, 'I'm pleased, of course. Pleased *enough*. As pleased as is warranted. But honestly, Lizzie – the rest of you, not to say *tout le monde*, seem so inordinately pleased with Gideon that – good God – I mean – there he is: hasn't lifted a finger, properly speaking, except in pursuit of the devices and desires of his own heart, with the result that he's got you all dancing around him like courtiers – The Fox, Auntie Beeb, *Times*, *Telegraph* and *Guardian* – what a shenanigans – all I can say is, it just seems to me absurdly unfair.'

'Well,' said Lizzie through her laughter, 'now you, too, know all about life. It's unfair.'

'*Touché*,' said Alfred. 'Damn it.'

48

'Kid get off all right?'

'Oh, yes. Home and dry, as we speak. I telephoned the other evening.'

Mimi had been returned to sender some days previously; Andrew and Alex were drinking the post-squash beers; catching up. Taking stock.

'Everything go well, then?'

Andrew drank, considering the question. 'As well as could be hoped,' he said. 'She seems to have a reasonably good grasp of the situation.'

'She's quite happy, then?'

'Happy enough. As far as I can tell. Yes – I'd say she's happy.'

'What is she now, six?'

'Seven. Old enough to think.'

They considered the thinking capacities of the seven-year-old. 'Yes,' said Alex. 'I should have thought so.'

'I'll have to try and get over there at Christmas time. For a few weeks, at any rate.'

'There's a good idea.'

'Yes.' What else to say, on this topic? Andrew's sorrow, his stoicism, his honourable intentions, were all beyond the reach of comment. 'Marriage, eh?' said Alex. 'You might as well walk across a minefield blindfolded.'

Andrew laughed very briefly. 'Probably,' he said. 'Still, as long as the kid's all right.' Alex thought about this. 'So you'd say,' he said, slowly, 'that children aren't too badly affected by divorce, would you? That is – Mimi at any rate, seems to be all right: so for all we know—'

'Well, everything depends on the particular circumstances, I suppose,' said Andrew. 'I mean, if the decision had been mine alone, or even chiefly mine, I dare say I mightn't have taken the risk: but as it was, Janet simply took the matter out of my hands, so I had no choice. Had to get on and make the best of it. Perhaps we've just been lucky, with Mimi. In any case, it's early days yet.'

'Yes,' said Alex. 'Still—'

'As a matter of fact, these studies of the effects of divorce on children—'

'Yes.'

'—universally agreed to be deleterious, to put it no worse—'

'Yes—'

'—are actually pretty worthless.'

'Are they?'

'Well, it's not as if these surveys are, or even can be, scientific.'

'No, I suppose not.'

'We don't know how miserable or how maladjusted the same children would have been if the parents had stayed together.'

'No, I suppose we don't.'

'So one has to take one's chances.'

'All the same, as you said – if it had been up to you—'

'Well, you know what we're like. Blokes like us. We were brought up to believe – to know for a fact – that if a certain course of action seemed alluring, it was probably – or even certainly – wrong. So, leaving one's partner – especially for another more agreeable one – is always going to look dodgy, isn't it?'

''Fraid so.'

'And who's to know,' said Andrew, unsmiling, 'that it isn't, after all?'

'Who, indeed?'

'You pays your money.'

Alex was silent. Andrew drank again. 'It's impossible, really. We're all just stumbling around in the dark. We can't possibly know what we're doing – not really. We just do the best we can.'

'For what that's worth.'

'As you say.'

They sat there, each momentarily tasting the sensation, here and now, of being the hero of such a tale – improvised, inglorious, inconclusive and ultimately, after all (unless you believed in a Divine Purpose), meaningless. Andrew thought fleetingly of Barbara, now in his memory another item in the account of loss and sorrow. He didn't know now even where she was precisely – the Harbour Bridge postcard of a few months past had been her last communication.

Alex also thought of Barbara, for whom the waiting – as a conscious, active, lively state – was done. To think of Barbara, now, was intemperately to invite mere hopeless anguish. Alex, these days, avoided thinking of Barbara.

'After all, it's not our fault,' said Andrew, 'that we're ignorant and inept – it's the way we're designed, basically. Not our fault.'

'No, you're right. Not our fault at all. Even we can see that far into it.'

'After all, as a species, we're still in the experimental stage.'

'I would have thought so.'

'It's obvious. Haven't clocked up so much as our first million years, even. Not even our first *half* million, by all accounts.'

'No. *Long* way to go.'

'Hope they're going to appreciate what we've gone through for them, we prototypes of *homo sapiens*.'

'Probably won't. Probably just take their perfect lives completely for granted.'

'Absurd, isn't it? Probably won't even be speaking English.'

'Oh, come now: of course they'll be speaking English. In a somewhat altered form, no doubt. But it's absolutely bound to be English.'

'You think?'

'Sure of it.'

'Think they'll play cricket?'

'Of course.'

'Football, obviously.'

'Obviously.'

'Still, they'll never know—'

'No; they never will.'

They each thought about what these remote successors would never know. 'Hardly worth being human, really, in that case,' said Andrew, after a while. 'No,' said Alex. 'Utterly pointless, really.'

49

Marguerite, at the great age of eleven, a reserved and rather fragile-looking child with dark brown hair, knew many things.

A large proportion of these many were unaccountable, were phenomena which, having no evident heads or tails of cause and consequence, were unclassifiable. She hardly knew or remembered how some of them had come to her knowledge – some of them, indeed, seeming to have arrived there entirely unbidden.

All such unaccountable matter, whatever its origin, having been turned over as well as could be managed, was thereafter filed away in the hope that it might be elucidated in due course: such marvels as sexual intercourse (why should anyone, ever, want to do *that*?) or the Trinity (how could anyone, whomsoever, believe what could not be understood?). And others, nearer to home, such as, that her parents did not love each other and would quite certainly – but when? – be divorced.

This item – which had come to her well over a year ago – was taken occasionally from the file marked 'to be elucidated' and pondered afresh, but to no avail. It was knowledge which must be harboured, simply, in silence and fear – fear, not so much of the eventuality itself, as that Percy too might awaken to it: for she did not consider that Percy would be as able as was she to accommodate it. Percy was not only younger but more erratic than she. You never knew what Percy might say, or do.

Percy's appearance was rather similar to his sister's. He had the same dark brown hair, the same thin, almost fragile, face: but his was adorned with a pair of wire-rimmed glasses of which he was rather proud. On first trying them on, he had been invited by the optician to look in the mirror and see how he liked them, Claire, who had taken him there, standing by. Percy gazed steadily for several seconds at his new reflection. Then he pronounced. 'They're good,' he said. 'They make me look as old as I feel.'

Percy was none the less forbidden to come home from school without Marguerite: forbidden so much as to leave the school grounds alone, because there was a five-to-ten-minute walk between the bus stop and home, and Percy was not to be in the streets alone – not until he was ten. Because, as Claire pointed out, over his protests, 'You're not as old as you feel.'

The two children generally walked home from the bus stop in silence to begin with, Percy, as he had lately learned to do, sauntering, his mind at work. Today, early in the new school year, his saunter slowed to an almost indolent gait, and he hunched his shoulders, casting his features into a morose expression. He was doing his new form teacher. Marguerite turned to him.

'Come on, Percy.'

He shrugged, returning to his own person, and quickened his pace very slightly, drawing almost level with his sister. 'I say, I've been thinking,' he announced. 'Have you?' 'Yes. Listen. I was just wondering – do you think they'll get divorced this year?'

Marguerite stopped walking for a moment: there was a nasty lurching feeling in her stomach. 'Who'll get divorced?' she said.

'Mum and Dad, of course. You know. Claire, and Alex.'

'Oh.'

The shock began, but very slowly, to abate. 'Well,' said Percy, almost impatiently, '*do* you?'

'I don't know.'

'No, of course you don't *know*, but do you *think*?'

The thing was, Percy's tone betrayed no distress, or even anxiety: he seemed simply to want to *know*: that was all. Glancing at his face, she saw the same Percy. Marguerite still felt a sort of trembling in her chest as she spoke, but she tried to seem quite as detached, quite as cool, as her brother.

'I don't know whether they'll get divorced this year, or any other year,' she said. 'Oh, they *will* get divorced, some year or other,' Percy assured her. 'I've been expecting it for a while. I was just wondering *when*, that's all.'

'I see,' said Marguerite dazedly. She was still trying to accommodate herself to this revised Percy. You never knew, indeed, what Percy would do, or say. 'I mean,' Percy expanded, 'they probably *should* get divorced, sooner or later. People do.'

'Not all people.' Marguerite still felt it best to respond as if quite ignorant, as if the topic were an absolute novelty. That did seem safest.

'Yes, okay, not all. But *they* ought to. I think they *will*.'

'Why do you think that?'

He seemed almost surprised at her asking, and almost stopped walking. 'Well, I dunno,' he said. He was now standing still, thinking; he was considering his parents. 'They're much *nicer*,' he said at last, 'when they're not together.' That was an indubitable, long-demonstrated, fact. There was no fun, no laughter, to be had with either but when the other was absent. It was like living in two – or rather, three – worlds, turn and turn about. Time with Claire; time with Alex; time with both of them present – he remote, she impatient – in the sober high-ceilinged house, where you knew, always, what came next.

'Yes,' said Marguerite, 'I suppose they are, actually.' Percy glanced quickly at her face. Had she really never considered all this before? Could she really be so ignorant? You couldn't be sure, with Marguerite: she was liable to conceal her feelings, her thoughts. 'I mean,' he urged, 'they just don't *get on*; they annoy each other. They get on each other's nerves. You must have *noticed*.' 'Yes,' said Marguerite, 'I suppose I had, sometimes.'

'*So?*'

'So what?'

'Shouldn't they get divorced? *Won't* they?'

'I suppose they might, one of these days.'

'Well – *when?*'

'How could I know?'

Percy thought for a minute. They were almost home. 'Perhaps we'd better ask them,' he said.

'We can't do that.'

'Why not?'

'I don't know – we just *can't*.'

'*I* can. I *will*. I want to know.'

She could see that he did, indeed. Oh, so did she – but –

'Percy, you *can't*. They wouldn't like it, I'm sure they wouldn't.'

'Why ever not?'

'I don't know – I just don't think they would.'

'Oh, I won't ask them both together, I'll just ask one. I'll ask Claire, while we're having tea.' They were turning in at their gate now, going up their path, ringing their doorbell. 'Perhaps she isn't there,' said Marguerite, desperately. 'Perhaps she's still out, perhaps it's only Mrs Brick.' When Claire was delayed, she would telephone Mrs Brick – if it was one of Mrs Brick's days – and ask her to stay on and mind the children until she got home. Oh, God, prayed Marguerite, let it be Mrs Brick. Then with any luck he might have forgotten about all this by the time Claire gets home. Please, God: please let it be Mrs Brick.

Percy pushed open the brass mail flap and peered through the slot to see whose feet should come down the hallway. 'Well, if it is Mrs Brick,' he said, still watching to see who was coming, 'I'll just have to wait until Claire gets home, that's all. What's the odds?' Then he saw, at last, who was coming. He straightened up, and turned to the terrified Marguerite. 'Guess who it is!' he said. 'Quick – guess who?' But it was too late to guess: the latch clicked, and the front door began – but slowly, heavily – to open.

A PURE CLEAR LIGHT
Madeleine St John

'A triumph of the minimalist, it appraises love,
both sacred and profane, desire, pain and the
disappointments of this earth with a laser eye.'
The Times

£5.99   1 85702 414 1

THE ESSENCE OF THE THING
Madeleine St John
Shortlisted for the 1997 Booker Prize

'There isn't a false note in the book, nothing but
ravishing grace, wit and tender feelings.'
Mail on Sunday

£6.99   1 85702 707 8

**All Fourth Estate books are available from your local bookshop,
or can be ordered direct from:**

**Fourth Estate, Book Service By Post, PO Box 29,
Douglas, I-O-M, IM99 1BQ**

Credit cards accepted.

**Tel: 01624 836000   Fax: 01624 670923
Internet: http://www.bookpost.co.uk
e-mail: bookshop@enterprise.net**

**Or visit the Fourth Estate website at:
www.4thestate.co.uk**

*Please state when ordering if you do **not** wish to receive further
information about Fourth Estate titles.*